She loosened the chain around her waist, letting its length trickle between her fingers into a small mound at the base of the pole.

The hook that secured her dress was next to go. With a shimmy, the gold lamé puddled at her feet, leaving her in a strapless black bra and thong. The act brought the usual reaction, still muted in her music-dazed brain…then her muscles went taut. A shiver rippled along her skin, making her feel *exposed,* and heat followed in its wake.

Opening her eyes, she searched for the gaze that could create such awareness, knowing that it was Rick's. He stood off to the side, leaning against the jamb, arms crossed over his chest. He looked formidable enough to be a bouncer and drop-dead sexy enough to be any woman's fantasy.

And he was watching her with enough intensity to maker her feel like *his* fantasy.

Dear Reader,

In the past few years, exotic dancing has become a whole lot more respectable. Women dance to stay in shape and to keep their marriages spicy; stripper poles are turning up in the homes of everyday people; classes are offered at gyms and as part of vacation packages—and wasn't that Oprah hosting a quick intro to stripping on her show?

So when I was working on the idea for this book, I wasn't surprised to find out that Amanda was a stripper. It wasn't something I chose for her; it was just part of who she was. I'd already set up Rick, an undercover agent for the Georgia Bureau of Investigation, as a bartender in a strip club. Since he would be working a lot in the book, wouldn't it be easier for his heroine to be someone he works with? And who better for a law-enforcing, badge-carrying investigator to fall in love with?

Love should never go *too* smoothly, now should it?

Marilyn Pappano

FORBIDDEN STRANGER

Marilyn Pappano

Silhouette®
Romantic
SUSPENSE

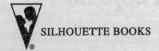

SILHOUETTE BOOKS

ISBN-13: 978-0-373-27565-6
ISBN-10:   0-373-27565-X

FORBIDDEN STRANGER

Copyright © 2008 by Marilyn Pappano

Printed in U.S.A.

Books by Marilyn Pappano

Silhouette Romantic Suspense

Michael's Gift #583
Regarding Remy #609
A Man Like Smith #626
Survive the Night #703
Discovered: Daddy #746
Convincing Jamey #812
The Taming of Reid Donovan #824
Knight Errant #836
The Overnight Alibi #848
Murphy's Law #901
**Cattleman's Promise #925
**The Horseman's Bride #957
**Rogue's Reform #1003
Who Do You Love? #1033
"A Little Bit Dangerous"
My Secret Valentine #1053

**The Sheriff's Surrender #1069
The Princess and
  the Mercenary #1130
**Lawman's Redemption #1159
**One True Thing #1280
**The Bluest Eyes in Texas #1391
Somebody's Hero #1427
More Than a Hero #1453
One Stormy Night #1471
Forbidden Stranger #1495

*Southern Knights
**Heartbreak Canyon

MARILYN PAPPANO

brings impeccable credentials to her career—a lifelong habit of gazing out windows, not paying attention in class, daydreaming and spinning tales for her own entertainment. The sale of her first book brought great relief to her family, proving that she wasn't crazy but was, instead, creative. Since then, she's sold more than forty books to various publishers and has even sold her work to a film production company.

She writes in an office nestled among the oaks that surround her home. In winter she stays inside with her husband and their four dogs, and in summer she spends her free time mowing the yard, which never stops growing, and daydreams about grass that never gets taller than two inches. You can write to her at P.O. Box 643, Sapulpa; OK 74067-0643.

Chapter 1

At 1:55 a.m., Amanda Nelson finished her last dance. After stopping in the dressing room to pull jeans and a T-shirt over her hot pink bra and Brazilian thong and to replace six-inch heels with flip-flops, she was out the back door by 2:01, keys in hand, way past ready to go home.

There were still customers in the club, finishing one last drink, some of them trying to buy companionship for the rest of the night from the girls willing to be bought. Those who weren't willing were still in the dressing room, unwinding, taking off stage makeup, making plans to go out and party. Amanda was the only one in the shadowy parking lot behind the club. That fact creeped her out and made her walk a little faster, clench the keys a little tighter. She had strong lungs and stronger legs, as well as a container of pepper spray in her purse, but she didn't want to be forced into a test of her ability to defend herself.

She was only a few yards from her car when a shadow separated from the darkness and moved toward her. Her heart jumped and her throat tightened in the instant before she recognized him.

Rick Calloway, part-time bartender, full-time hunk. He'd been at Almost Heaven only a few weeks, and that was all the girls knew about him. Well, that, plus the fact that he was the epitome of tall, dark and handsome.

But Amanda wasn't just one of the girls. She knew Rick was six years older than her, that he came from the small Georgia town of Copper Lake, that the crook in his nose was the result of a high-school brawl, that he had two brothers, Robbie and Russ. She also knew that he hadn't recognized her or her name, and for that she was grateful. Growing up in Copper Lake was an experience she preferred to leave in the past.

"Hey, Amanda. Sorry if I startled you."

"You didn't," she lied. She used the remote to unlock her car, the headlights automatically flashing, illuminating him for a few seconds. He wore jeans, faded and snug, and an emerald-green polo shirt, also snug. His dark hair curled over his collar, and his olive-toned skin was stubbled with beard along his jaw. His eyes were surprisingly blue, like Robbie's, and his voice sounded enough like Robbie's had fifteen years ago that she would need more than a few words to tell them apart.

In his two weeks at the club, he hadn't spoken to her more than a few times, and then only to steer her toward a customer who was dropping big bucks. She'd spoken to him only to thank him with a share of her tip. She never got cozy with the guys at work, neither the managers nor the employees nor the customers. She particularly didn't want to get cozy with Robbie Calloway's brother.

After tossing her gym bag into the backseat, she turned to face him. "Is there something I can do for you?"

"Yeah." He shifted awkwardly. In all the times she'd seen him, awkward hadn't been his style. "I have a friend who, uh, wants to learn to dance. I was wondering if—" he shrugged "—if you'd teach her."

Amanda had always been a dancer. Her earliest memories were of twirling around the living room, alone or in her father's arms, while her mother watched with an indulgent smile. Then the accident had happened and her father never twirled her nor her mother indulged her again.

She'd never had a lesson. She didn't bother with routines, didn't care about choreography. Moving to music came naturally to her. What little training she'd gotten had been on the job: watching the other dancers at that first club, getting a feel for what the customers liked and making it her own.

"There are classes she can take," she said at last.

"She's a little shy."

"She can buy a videotape."

"She does better with hands-on instruction."

"Does she want to do this as a job or just for you?"

With the only light coming from the nearest streetlamp, it was impossible to say for sure, but his cheeks seemed darker. His voice was definitely a shade hoarser. "Uh, both, I think."

Stripping could certainly bring a shy woman out of her shell. Not that Amanda knew from experience. She'd never had a shy bone in her body, her father used to say. She'd always been brash and bold, going after what she wanted. She still pursued her goals, but the brashness and boldness had worn off after twelve years on the club circuit.

"I'd pay for your time, of course," Rick said.

She smiled thinly. Money—the magic word. Every exotic dancer she knew was in it for the money. It was a job that always outdid minimum wage and, if a girl was lucky and stayed in good shape, sometimes paid extraordinarily well. The trick was to put some of the good money away to help out through the not-so-good times.

That was a lesson Amanda had learned early on. She'd paid for her car with her savings, bought a house and put herself through college. When her thirty-first birthday rolled around in six weeks, she would officially retire from the business. No more bikini waxes, diets, working nights and sleeping days. No worrying about her body mass index or jogging three miles daily in Atlanta's muggy heat. No wearing clothes that wouldn't adequately cover a toddler—

Rick cleared his throat and she refocused on the subject. Did she want to teach Rick Calloway's girlfriend how to turn him on by taking off her clothes? Not particularly. Was she willing to take his money in exchange for a few hours of her free time? Why not? It wasn't as if she would be spending time with him. He would remain just as clueless about her as he was now.

"Okay. Tell her to call me." Climbing into her car, she

started the engine, then backed out. When she drove away, he was still standing there in the parking lot, watching her car as it disappeared into the night.

It was a ten-minute drive to her neighborhood, where her house stood in counterpoint to all the white houses on the block. Its wood siding was the color of a pumpkin pie fresh from the oven, its trim the same hue as whipped cream. It was small, little more than thirteen hundred square feet, but came with a decent-sized yard and a big front porch. And it was hers. Until she'd bought it, she'd never really had a place that was hers.

She parked in the driveway, then climbed the steps to the porch. It was deep enough to provide a sheltered view of the frequent summer storms and held a swing, a pine rocker, three wicker chairs and matching tables. With the floral cushions and the potted flowers scattered around, it was the fussiest space in her house.

Like her, the house was a work in progress; unlike her, it would soon be finished. She'd done the labor herself—hauling out cheap carpet and pad, stripping the heart of pine floors, sanding and refinishing them. She'd hung Sheetrock, replaced molding, completely retiled the fireplace surround, the kitchen and the bathroom. The only room left to finish was her bedroom, which would be done about the time she retired from dancing and started her new life.

Her puppy greeted her with a sleepy one-eyed look before rising to her feet, stretching, then padding over for a scratch. Amanda obliged her for a moment, then opened the door so Dancer could trot out into the yard.

In a minute or so, she was back, tail wagging lazily as she headed for her spot on the bed.

Stifling a yawn, Amanda wandered into her bedroom, still a ghastly "before" that would soon become a fresh "after." Not that there was a rush. She hadn't brought anyone home to see it in more months than she wanted to recall.

And that admission was certainly no reason for Rick Calloway's image to pop into her mind. She'd had enough of the Calloways to last a lifetime. Her father had worked for Calloway Industries, as his father and grandfather had. They'd lived in houses and apartments owned by the Calloways, had shopped in Calloway stores in a town whose mayor was always a Calloway. Her own first job had been for the family, and her first broken heart had come at the hands of Robbie Calloway. When she'd left Copper Lake almost fifteen years ago, she'd thought she'd seen the last of them.

Then Rick Calloway had walked into the club. There was no mistaking that he was one of *those* Calloways. She may not have seen one in ages, but the family resemblance was strong. She'd held her breath for a time, hoping he wouldn't recognize her before realizing her own conceit. He'd never noticed her when they lived in the same small town. He'd been older, she'd been poorer; he'd been special, she'd been nobody. How could he recognize someone he hadn't known existed?

Giving in to a yawn, she kicked off her shoes and went into the bathroom, the tile cold beneath her feet. While the tub filled with hot water, she stripped off her clothes, removed her makeup and secured her hair to the top of her head before sliding into the tub. There was a time when she'd danced a six- or eight-hour shift, then gone out to party for another three hours. Not anymore. Stripping was a demanding job that took its toll on a body. A dancer had only so many good years and she was at the end of hers.

Her new career wouldn't be nearly as strenuous. Walking across campus, carrying books, handing out stacks of papers… Eyes closed, she smiled, her satisfaction so intense that the water around her practically vibrated with it. Amanda Nelson, poor girl who would never amount to anything, high school dropout, stripper, was going back to college.

This time as a teacher.

For the first time in her life, she was going to be one hundred percent respectable.

If he were alive today, wouldn't her father be proud?

Bleary-eyed after less than five hours' sleep, Rick Calloway slid into the booth across from his sometimes-partner and removed his sunglasses. He winced at the bright light and put them on again, then took a swig of coffee. What it lacked in heat, it more than made up for in bitterness, but he didn't bother doctoring it. He wouldn't bother finishing it, either.

"You look like you had a tough night." Julia Dautrieve's voice was just like her—no-nonsense. Everything about her was function over style, from her black dress with matching jacket to her low-heeled shoes. She was smart as hell, handled a gun better than most of the men they worked with and was more capable than just about anyone he knew. He just couldn't see her handling this new job.

"My night would have been fine if someone hadn't dragged me out of bed at an ungodly hour for coffee," he grumbled. The club closed at two, but by the time he got everyone out so he could clean and lock up, it was usually after three. This morning it had been four before he'd made it home, five before he'd showered and fallen asleep.

Thinking about Amanda Nelson.

He'd noticed her his first night on the job. Hell, he was alive, wasn't he? Five foot six, slender as a reed but with some very nice curves, too. Long auburn hair that curled wildly, endless legs, pale golden skin. And she'd been showing a lot of skin that first night, wearing a tiny yellow bra that covered only the necessities and a breakaway skirt that was about the size of a paper towel.

It had been clear that night that she was a lot of guys' fantasy come to life, but not his. She was part of the job and Harry had told him with a wink and a grin, "Look, but don't touch." That was official policy at all the clubs, though it was broken at all of them. He hadn't yet met the bartender, bouncer or manager who hadn't had a thing with one or more of the girls at their clubs.

Look, but don't touch was *his* official policy. His bosses at the Georgia Bureau of Investigation would frown on him hooking up with a stripper while in the course of his investigation.

"Did you talk to her?"

Julia's businesslike tone cut into his thoughts and made him scowl. "Yeah. She said okay."

"Damn." Julia's voice held more emotion than usual—disappointment, irritation. "I was hoping…"

That Amanda would turn him down. That all the girls would tell him no, earning Julia a reprieve. Amanda had agreed for a price, though they hadn't settled on an amount yet. Most of the dancers at Almost Heaven would have agreed for free—at least, for no cash payment. Most of them had already come on to him.

Except Amanda.

"You can tell Baker you won't do it."

Now it was her turn to scowl. "I've never backed away from a challenge. I can't afford to."

Being a woman in a still predominantly male field probably did have its challenges. Rick wondered if that was the reason for the ugly shoes, the plain clothes, the severe hair. Was this her way of making her gender less of an issue, or was she stuffy and uptight by nature? He'd worked with her for three years, but didn't know. Didn't know much at all about her personal life. He'd asked. She'd just never answered.

"He can't make you go undercover as a stripper."

Julia shrugged. "It's just part of the job. No big deal." Then she slid her cell phone across the table. "Call her. Set up an appointment."

Rick ignored her phone and pulled his out instead. Before leaving the club that morning, he'd put Amanda's number in his phone book. She would think he'd gotten it from Harry, which suited him just fine. None of the girls needed to know that GBI had done background investigations on them all.

As the phone rang, he idly wondered if it was too

early to call. She'd left the club two hours before him, but that didn't mean she'd gone home and to bed. She could have stopped for something to eat, gone out with friends or had a date. Not his business if she had.

But she answered on the third ring and her voice was too cheerful and alert for her to have been sleeping. The simple sound of her hello conjured an image of her, not in the skimpy clothes he usually saw her in, but the way she'd looked that morning, in faded jeans and a T-shirt advertising Atlanta's zoo. She'd looked so different. Still pretty, still sexy, just wholesome. Unjaded.

She'd repeated the *hello* before he prodded himself to answer. "Hey, this is Calloway. Did I wake you?"

"No, not at all."

"I told Julia, my, uh, friend, that you'd agreed to teach her, and she wanted to know when you could start."

Her voice hushed, Amanda spoke to someone in the background, and Rick wondered again if she'd had a date and if he'd slept over. What kind of man dated a stripper? Not that there was anything wrong with strippers in general. Most of them he'd met were nice women just trying to make their way. But what kind of man didn't mind that his girlfriend took off her clothes for the gratification of strangers? Maybe Rick was old-fashioned, but he liked to believe that, when he was involved with a woman, he was the only one seeing her naked, or practically so.

"Sorry," Amanda said into the phone. "My puppy was trying to eat my laundry. Um, is she available today?"

Today? Rick mouthed, and Julia mouthed back, *Now?* "How about now?" he asked.

"Sure, anytime. I'll be here until six-thirty. My address is…"

Rick didn't pay much attention. He'd already gotten that from her file, too. He was thinking about the fact that it was a puppy, not a boyfriend, who'd distracted her, and the fact that the knowledge was somehow satisfying when it shouldn't mean a damn thing.

"Okay," he said when she stopped talking. "I'll tell her. Thanks."

Julia waited until he'd flipped shut the phone. "Well?"

"Anytime before six-thirty. She's working tonight." Working. Dancing. Taking off her clothes. She was one of the few dancers at Almost Heaven who didn't strip down to nothing but a thong or g-string. She always kept those teeny-tiny bras on, and the men didn't mind, always tipping her generously.

But there wasn't a man among them who didn't wish she would dispose of the bra just once.

"Are you going with me?" Julia asked.

"Why?"

"Just to perform the introductions." She was uncharacteristically nervous—her gaze not quite meeting his, her fingers pressing against the coffee cup hard enough to turn the tips white.

"Okay. Sure." He wouldn't mind seeing where Amanda lived. Seeing how she looked on a normal day when she was just being herself and not an exotic dancer whose job was to titillate.

Then he would go home and back to bed for a few hours' more sleep.

Julia left enough money to cover the coffee, then slid

out of the booth. Her shoulders were set, the line of her spine rigid. He couldn't imagine her loosening up enough to mimic even one of Amanda's fluidly sensual, graceful moves, but she might surprise him. As she'd said, she didn't back away from a challenge.

He gave her the address in case they got separated, then climbed into his car. The engine growled to life, vibrating through the seat. The Calloway boys all had a thing for old engines with power. His 1969 Camaro was a couple years older than him, with a 454-cubic-inch small block V8 that put out 641 horsepower. It was *fast*.

With Julia following in her sedan—good price, good mileage, so-so performance, totally forgettable—he navigated through mile after mile of gas stations, fast-food restaurants and used-car lots before turning into Amanda's neighborhood. The houses were older, probably built in the forties or fifties, most pretty well maintained. Hers stood out, sporting recent coats of orange and off-white paint that looked better than they should have. The grass was neatly mowed and the last of the summer flowers bloomed along the sidewalk and in beds that fronted the porch.

"It's a homey place for a stripper," Julia murmured when she got out of her car, parked at the curb behind his.

"You were expecting something a little more club-like? Or just a little more sinnerlike?" When she scowled at him, he grinned back. "Don't be disappointed yet. She might have the inside all done up in red and black satin with mirrors, poles and chains."

As they crossed the sidewalk, he took her arm. She stiffened but didn't pull away. "What's that for?"

"Didn't I tell you?" They climbed the steps and he rang the doorbell, then grinned at her again. "Amanda thinks you're wanting to learn to strip for me."

Color flooded Julia's face, but before she could say anything, the door opened. Amanda stood just inside the screen door, long curls pulled up in a ponytail, wearing a faded University of Georgia T-shirt, a pair of denim shorts, no shoes and no makeup. She looked younger than the thirty he knew her to be, soft and pretty and not the least exotic.

Beside her stood a dog the size of a small pony, long, gangly, with feet that would do an elephant proud. Its coat was pure black, sleek except for the cowlick between its ears, and its dark eyes were fixed on Rick. "Some 'puppy,'" he murmured.

"The vet estimates her age at about ten months. That makes you a puppy, doesn't it, Dancer?" Amanda unlatched the screen door, then stepped back. "Come on in. You must be Rick's friend. I'm Amanda Nelson."

"Julia Dautrieve." Giving the dog a wary look, Julia moved into the foyer, belatedly shaking hands with Amanda. She took a few steps away, glanced around, then smiled nervously. "I, uh, appreciate your doing this."

"No problem." Amanda shifted her gaze to Rick. He knew from her background investigation that she had hazel eyes. That seemed such a tame description for the blue, green and brown mix that gazed at him. "Are you going to stay?"

"No," he and Julia said at the same time. It was one thing to watch Amanda dance at the club, another to do so in the intimacy of her home, and still another to do

so with his supposed girlfriend there. He would be safer
all around if he left. Now.

"Julia's going to surprise me later," he said, making
his partner blush again. She really would surprise him
if she found the courage—and the sensuality—to go
through with the job. "I just came along to perform the
introductions. Now I'm outta here."

Amanda nodded, then went into the living room to
the right, giving him privacy to say goodbye to Julia.
He grasped her fingers, cold and clammy, and pulled
her around so his back was to Amanda. "You okay?"
he murmured.

Looking anything but, she nodded.

Not sure whether Amanda was watching, he brushed
a kiss across Julia's mouth. "Call me," he said, then
winked and grinned. "Have fun."

Before she could react—a forced smile, a sarcastic
reply, an internal struggle not to draw her weapon on
him—he ducked out the door, trotted along the sidewalk
to his car and slid behind the wheel. As he pulled away
from the curb, he felt a rush of relief, as if he'd just
escaped some danger.

And its name was Amanda.

Until the wee hours of that morning, Amanda hadn't
spent even one second considering what kind of woman
would attract Rick Calloway. As long as he paid no
attention to her, that was all that mattered. In the past
few hours, though, she'd wasted far too much time considering it, and she hadn't guessed even faintly close.

She'd expected someone pretty, sexy, maybe even

edgy. Someone sure of herself personally, professionally, sexually. Someone other guys would covet, who made other women feel insecure.

Not someone like Julia Dautrieve. Oh, she was attractive in a plain sort of way. She needed a more flattering hairstyle and the unrelenting black she wore made her porcelain complexion look pasty and washed out. The below-the-knee dress length was dowdy, and those shoes… Amanda's only thought on the shoes was *burn them*.

But she'd caught Rick's eye.

She was standing in the living room doorway, her gaze returning repeatedly to the stripper pole in the dining room, looking as if she'd like nothing more than to run in those sturdy, plain shoes back to her sturdy, plain car and her sturdy, plain world. But she hadn't fled yet, so Amanda chose to act as if she wouldn't.

"Would you like a glass of tea before we start?"

"I'd rather have scotch," Julia muttered.

"Sorry. I don't drink."

Julia smiled unsteadily. "Tea is fine."

"We can sit on the porch if you'd like. I think it's cool enough to be comfortable."

With a nod, Julia went outside. Nosing the screen door open, Dancer followed her while Amanda went to the kitchen for the tea. She carried the two glasses outside a moment later, finding Julia in one of the wicker chairs, Dancer in another. She handed one glass of tea to the woman, then took the third chair.

"Rick says you're interested in making a career change. What do you do now?"

"I'm a bookkeeper." Julia's nose wrinkled. "Big switch, huh?"

"Not really." Amanda was a stripper about to become a college-level English instructor. *That* was a big change. "Have you ever danced?"

"I took ballet when I was a kid."

"Really." Amanda never would have guessed it, except that she did have perfect posture. But no grace, no elegance, no comfort with her body.

Her noncommittal response didn't fool Julia. "I know. You'd never know it to look at me, would you?" She ran one fingernail along the rounded neckline of her dress as if it choked. "I'm a little uptight."

Amanda smiled gently. "I think when it comes to keeping books, being uptight is probably a good thing."

"Probably, but it doesn't do much for a woman."

Didn't do much for Rick? Was that what she meant?

Gazing at the periwinkles that bordered the porch, Amanda asked, "What made you decide to try this?" If she was forcing herself to act so totally out of character for anyone besides herself, it wasn't going to work. Like losing weight or getting in shape, stripping was something a woman had to want for herself.

"Oh, I don't know. I think every woman must wonder what it would be like." Julia shrugged uncomfortably. "Wearing sexy clothes, doing sexy dances, having men look at you, want you, pay to be with you. Men have probably always looked at you like that, but not me. I just want to know how it feels."

How it felt was unremarkable. Just as balancing spreadsheets was part of Julia's day, it was part of the job.

Oh, not in the beginning. There had been a real sense of power in those early days. Men who had never laid eyes on her before were willing to pay money just to have her sit at their tables and talk to them—willing to pay a lot of money for private dances. They hadn't known or cared that she'd grown up on the wrong side of town, that she'd gone through a wild-child phase in high school, that the boys back home had called her Randy Mandy. All they'd cared about was those few minutes when her attention was all theirs.

"But you have a boyfriend that most of the girls at the club would give a month's worth of tips to have for just one night," Amanda pointed out.

For a moment, Julia looked puzzled, then she gave a shake of her head as if clearing it. "You mean Rick. Yeah, he's a nice guy."

Funny. "Nice" didn't come to mind first, second or even third when Amanda thought of Rick—or any other Calloway, for that matter. Handsome, sexy, privileged, snobbish, bastard—at least, when it came to Robbie.

"Did he ask you to do this?"

Pink tinged Julia's cheeks. No doubt, she hated to blush, but there were men at the club who would pay extra just to see it. Innocence fascinated them, especially when they saw so little of it onstage. "No," she denied unconvincingly. "I want to give it a shot. See if it will help me loosen up." She took a deep breath, then her pretty brown gaze met Amanda's. "I've been rigid and stuffy all my life. Just once I'd like to be something else."

Amanda understood wanting to be something else. She'd felt the yearning, the need, the dissatisfaction.

"All right. Let's go inside and start turning you into something else."

Julia was slow to rise from the chair. As she did, Dancer jumped to the floor, too, trotted over and walked through the open screen door, stopped at the water dish, then curled onto the one-armed chaise that served as Amanda's sofa.

"I like your house," Julia said as she followed Amanda down the hall and into the bedroom.

"Thank you. I did it—am doing it—myself." She pointed to the chair in front of her dressing table, then slapped down a packet of makeup remover towelettes. "Take off your makeup."

The dressing table was really an old rolltop desk, with a lighted makeup mirror in the center and everything a woman needed to make herself look good tucked into the drawers and cubbies. Amanda plugged in the curling iron, used in the occasional futile attempt to tame her own curls, then began removing the pins that held Julia's hair in its unforgiving chignon.

"You realize your age will work against you," she commented as she combed out the fine silken strands. "Twenty-nine, thirty—that's pretty much the cutoff for dancers. It's a hard job."

"I know. I'm not giving up my day job. I'd just like to do it for a while."

"And Rick's okay with that."

"Sure. Why wouldn't he be? Your boyfriends don't mind, do they?"

Amanda combed out a section of silky black hair, then rolled it onto the curling iron. "They usually didn't mind in the beginning. Sooner or later, though, they got jealous." Or, worse, they got turned on—not by her, her dancing, her body, but by the fact that *other* men were turned on by her. The ick factor in that was too extreme to overcome.

But she'd thought Rick… Hell, she didn't *know* Rick. And he was Robbie's brother, after all. His ick factor could well be much higher than she wanted to know.

Face stripped clean of makeup, Julia watched silently as Amanda curled her hair. Finally, almost timidly, she said, "I thought you'd teach me something today."

"You want things to be different. We're starting with making you look different. Your hair is too stuffy and your makeup's too subtle." Amanda smiled a bit wistfully. "There's nothing subtle about this business."

Leaving the curled hair to cool, she turned her attention to makeup. Her skin tone was a few shades darker than Julia's, but with some mixing of foundations, she matched it pretty closely. Judging by the faint smears on the towelette, Julia's normal routine included foundation, blush and a single shade of eye shadow, all applied with a very light touch. Her eyes popped when she got a look at the products Amanda lined up, everything from corrector to eyeliner to glimmery powder.

"A lot of new dancers take a drink or two before they go onstage," she remarked as she worked. "It becomes a habit way too easily, so don't even start. And take the time to find some good body makeup. If you do much floor or pole work, you'll need it to cover the bruises. Buy your shoes now and get used to wearing them. You're about my height, so four-inch heels are the minimum. Try the six-inch, and when you can handle them, consider the eight-inch. They make your legs and your butt look better and that will get you better tips."

"Eight-inch heels?" Julia squeaked. "I wear flats."

"Not to dance. You'll have to invest in some clothes, too—thongs, bras, skirts, booty shorts. There's a little shop here in town—" Amanda broke off when a giggle escaped Julia.

"Booty shorts?" she echoed.

"Micro shorts, hipsters. Just like you CPA types, we have our own lingo. For your first time out, I'd recommend a Brazilian thong. It gives more coverage in back than a regular thong. And you know you have to have a bikini wax."

"That's one thing that's not new," Julia said with a grimace.

Maybe she wasn't as ill-suited to this adventure as she seemed. Once Amanda retired, she would give up bikinis forever, because she was damn sure giving up bikini waxes. She was getting rid of all her dance clothes and her arch-killing shoes—well, there was one pair of sweet crystal-encrusted four-and-a-half-inch stilettos that made her legs to die for. And maybe she'd keep the Tinkerbell skirt with its fluttery hem and the iridescent bra that matched. After all, she was giving up stripping, not looking sexy from time to time.

She dusted a mocha-hued eyeshadow over Julia's lids before picking up the gel eyeliner and a small brush. "If you want to dance professionally for any length of time, you'll have to get in better shape. Jogging is great for stamina, and weight-training to define the muscles.

Yoga, too. It gives you a longer, leaner look. And watch your diet. Low carbs, low fat, low calorie. The lower your body fat, the bigger your tips."

"Jeez, this sounds like training for some sort of athletic competition."

"It is," Amanda agreed. More than most people realized. But dancers didn't get the kind of respect athletes did—at least, not exotic dancers. To too many people, strippers were one step, if even that, above prostitutes. She'd never had sex for money, but her aunt Dana had still called her a whore when she'd thrown Amanda out of her house twelve years ago. Her mother had still talked about the shame she'd felt when Amanda had decided to make her temporary dance job permanent.

Her hand trembled, smearing the black-brown mascara. She used a swab to clean away the streak, then concentrated on what she was doing. Those old hurts would never be gone. She could haul them out to reexamine tomorrow or next month. At the moment, though, she had a job to do.

Taking money from Rick Calloway to make his girlfriend sexier for him.

Just like her father and her mother before her, she was working for a Calloway. But this was different. Her parents had worked for the Calloways because they'd owned damn near everything in Copper Lake. They'd had no choice. In this venture, all the choices were Amanda's. Her livelihood wasn't at stake. All she had to say was no, and their association would end.

When she finished with the makeup, she combed out Julia's curls before letting her check the results in the mirror. Julia's brown eyes widened as she turned her head from side to side. "Oh, my gosh. I look…"

Her black hair shimmered in waves that softened her face, and the makeup played up her eyes and the great cheekbones beneath them. She looked prettier, more approachable, sexier.

"Wow. This is worth whatever Rick's paying you. I could stop right now—" Abruptly, she bit her lip, smudging the lip liner/lipstick/lip gloss Amanda had just applied. After a moment, she smiled and went on with less enthusiasm. "I'm just kidding. Of course I want to learn to dance. I really do."

Who was she trying to convince? Amanda?

Or herself?

Chapter 2

Rick stood behind the bar, damp cloth in hand, tooth-pick between his teeth. He glanced at his watch. It was eight-thirty. Amanda had finished her first set fifteen minutes ago and was now seated at a stage-side table with some of her regulars. Four men, early fifties to sixties, varying shades of gray except for one bald guy, always dressed in suits and ties. They looked just like the businessmen that made up about half the clientele, but he knew from the records checks that their business was education. Baldy was the president of a small liberal arts college nearby, and the other three were deans. Tuesday nights were their regular budget com-mittee meetings, or so they told their wives.

Rick hadn't talked to Amanda since he'd left her house that morning, but he'd spoken to Julia on the phone. She'd been pretty closed-mouthed about her first lesson, saying nothing besides it had gone well. Now she was in the process of moving into his apartment, halfway between Amanda's house and the club. She didn't like the idea, even though she would have her own room, but she damn sure didn't want to give out her real address when she came to work here. If she came to work here.

Amanda's laughter separated from the background noise, drawing his attention her way. She was standing now, one hand on the back of baldy's chair. Tonight the thong and bra were black-and-gold tiger stripes. Points of see-through black fabric fluttered over her middle and a length of shiny gold coiled around her upper left arm. The whole outfit was sexy, but just that bracelet wrapped around her bicep was enough to turn a man on.

She patted baldy on the shoulder, then headed toward the bar. Rick watched her, idly noting that the temperature seemed to be rising. Great for the girls in their skimpy costumes. In jeans and a T-shirt, he was liable to break out in a sweat.

Amanda stopped at the end of the bar. "Three vodka Collins, one cosmopolitan and a bottled water."

He got the water first, sliding it across the bar to her. It was tempting to stand there and watch her drink it— twist off the plastic cap, lift the bottle to her mouth, take a drink so long and so cold that it raised goose bumps on her skin. Instead, he turned his attention to the drinks. His only qualification for this job when he'd started was that he'd drunk his share of liquor over the years. A crash course in bartending, along with a tattered copy of *The Moron's Guide to Mixology* tucked under the bar, had gotten him through.

"Those men are old enough to be your grandfather," he remarked as he poured vodka into all four glasses.

"Father, actually. I'm not that young."

She looked way too young to be working in a place like this.

"Aren't you ever tempted to tell them to go home to their wives?"

She held the water bottle to her throat, close enough to feel the chill but not to touch her makeup. She had the makeup application down to an art—enough to look good under the stage lights, but not so much that it looked overdone offstage.

"Their wives don't miss them. The men have their budget committee meetings and the women have their garden club."

"Do they ever try to buy more than drinks?" None of his business, Rick silently acknowledged. Some dancers worked the prostitution angle; plenty didn't. When the case was over, he would put everything he'd found out in his report and if anyone on the job chose to pursue it, fine.

"Not these guys. Coming here is a little wild and risqué for them. Their lives are pretty tame."

Rick finished off the Collinses with club soda, then added triple sec, cranberry and lime juice to the cosmo. *Not these guys,* she'd said, which implied that others did. He wanted to ask which ones and whether they'd been successful. "How did it go with Julia?"

"Fine. We went shopping."

"I'm paying you to shop?"

The remark made her uneasy. Her gaze shifted away and it took a moment for her smile to form. "Great job, isn't it?" Then she shrugged, her tiger stripes rippling. "You can't dance without the right clothes and shoes."

He doubted most men would agree with her. The flashy colors and see-through fabrics were nice, but they weren't necessary. Every man he knew would be just as turned on by a woman wearing a white cotton bra and panties. In fact, Amanda, with her creamy golden skin, would look incredible in her underwear. There was something more intimate about imagining her in the lingerie she wore for herself, not for tips.

Wishing Harry would turn the AC to frigid, Rick set the last drink on her tray. "We never settled on an amount. How about one night's house fee per lesson?"

Her eyes widened slightly. One night on the stage cost each dancer seventy-five dollars. Anything over that, they got to pocket. Some girls actually went in the hole on slow nights, but weekends always made up for it.

"All right," she agreed. She picked up the tray and started away, then turned back. "You should have asked first. I would have settled for twenty-five, thirty bucks." She gracefully strolled away, tray balanced on one delicate hand.

When she was out of earshot, he murmured, "You would have sold yourself cheap, darlin'."

She was a beautiful woman. Smart. Capable. She could do anything she wanted, yet for twelve years she'd settled for this. Why?

He'd learned early in his career that asking why people did the things they did was an exercise in futility.

Why did a seventeen-year-old honor student decide the profit margin versus risk in selling drugs made it a good choice? Why did a gangbanger open fire on a crowd of strangers—kids, no less—as he drove down the street?

For the most part, Rick had lost interest in the why. His focus these days was on delivering the consequences to people who broke the law.

But he couldn't help but wonder about Amanda's why. Why was she a stripper? Why hadn't she pursued a more respectable career? Why wasn't she married and raising kids? Why was she spending her nights in a place like this with people like him?

The club had about two customers too many to rank as a slow night. Rick made drinks whose recipes he could now recite in his sleep, watched the customers and talked for a minute here or there with the dancers. It was casual conversation—drink orders, a little flirting. *You have any plans when you get off? Want to join me for dessert?* Unless he made an effort to see the girls outside the club—too risky—he had no real chance to get information from them. It was tough to subtly say, "A margarita on the rocks, a whiskey sour and, say, do you remember a girl named Lisa who used to work here?"

That was why Julia was coming onboard. Dancers talked to each other. Hopefully, they would talk to her about Lisa Howard, Tasha Wiley and DinaBeth Jones.

Three dancers, all having appeared on the main stage at Almost Heaven, all disappeared over a three-month period pretty much without a trace until parts from Tasha's and DinaBeth's cars had turned up in a chop shop on the northern side of Atlanta. The chop shop happened to belong to Roosevelt Hines, who also owned Almost Heaven and its four sister clubs.

Rosey, he called himself, and no one laughed. He stood six-six, weighed three hundred pounds and didn't give a damn about anyone but himself. He'd started with petty theft when he was ten and worked his way up the food chain. The strip clubs were the most legitimate of his businesses. He said he liked his girls, claimed he kept the bad stuff away from them.

Would Lisa, Tasha and DinaBeth agree?

"Hey, Calloway, time for a break."

He glanced up to find Chad, bouncer and relief bartender, standing at the other end of the bar, flirting with a little blonde named Dawn. Rick had walked in on them in the storeroom his first night on the job, in the men's room the next night. He'd seen enough to make a point of always knocking first.

There were dancers on all three stages, the budget committee was having a good time and there was no sign of Amanda. On her own break? Where Rick would have normally headed straight out back, this time he detoured past the dressing room. The door was always open; there was no false modesty among the dancers.

The room looked like an explosion of colors, leathers and metals. Bright lights circled the makeup mirrors and cosmetics spilled across the counters. Lockers lined one wall, holding the mundane jeans, T-shirts and running shoes that turned exotic dancers back into everyday young women.

Only one of the chairs in front of the mirrors was occupied, by a gorgeous Jamaican woman who was adding a coat of something to already-thick lashes. "Hey, sweetie," she greeted him. "You lookin' for some-one in particular, sugar? Or will Eternity do?"

She could ask that question of a thousand guys and get nothing but affirmation from every one of them. He grinned apologetically. "I wanted to ask Amanda something."

Her dark gaze narrowed. "Amanda, huh. I was betting Monique would be more your type. If Amanda's not out front, she's in study hall."

"Study hall?"

"That empty little room near the back door that no one ever uses."

"Thanks." He took a step out the door, then stopped. "Which one is Monique?"

"Brunette. Short hair. Triple D's."

Oh, yeah. There was a time when she would have been his type. A time all of them would have suited. "I have a girlfriend." It was a lie, but it sounded good.

Better to him than to Eternity, if her look was anything to judge by. "You think all them guys out there don't, chico?" she murmured as she turned back to her makeup.

Rick's jaw tightened as he followed the narrow hall to the rear of the building. He knew better than to equate a relationship with fidelity. His father had had a girl-friend or three, along with a wife. The only good thing Rick could say about the bastard was that he'd been discreet in his affairs. His mother hadn't had a clue until a heart attack had dropped the old man in his tracks and she'd found out that her sons had a half brother living down in Mississippi.

Sara had been a better woman than anyone had expected—than Gerald had deserved. She'd welcomed Mitch into the family and made a place for him in her own home. She loved him like one of her own. Too bad she'd loved Gerald, too.

Rick had been eleven when his father died and his mother's heart had been broken. He hadn't felt anything decent for Gerald since.

Reaching the closed door just ten feet from the rear exit, Rick knocked.

A moment later, the door swung open. "Getting formal, aren't we, Eternity? You always just barge— Oh. Sorry. No one usually bothers me back here be- sides—" Hugging her arms across her middle, Amanda finished with a grimace.

He would have invited himself inside if the space hadn't been so small or the idea hadn't seemed so bad. Instead, he leaned against the doorjamb and gave the room a quick scan. The walls were painted the same shade as her living room and the one-armed sofa looked a match to the one he'd seen at her place. There was an oval mirror on one wall, a floor lamp and a small table that held a bottle of water, a clock, a book, a pair of reading glasses and the empty wrapper from a trick-or- treat-size candy bar.

"Study hall?" he asked, bringing his gaze back to her.

She glanced at the table, too. "When I was in school, I studied in here on breaks."

"Getting your GED?"

A pained look slid across her face. "About eleven years ago. This summer I finished my bachelor's degree."

"Congratulations," he said, then added, "Sorry. I didn't mean…"

She shrugged. "A lot of us didn't get to finish high school."

But that was no reason to automatically assume she hadn't.

She'd traded tiger stripes for a filmy gold Grecian goddess thing that left one shoulder bare. She'd kept the gold coil around her arm. Her hair was piled on top of her head, curls spilling down, with a gold patterned band circling her forehead. Fabric draped loosely over her breasts, then gathered at her waist, belted by a thin gold chain. The skirt was barely deserving of the name, short, insubstantial, revealing peeks of the black thong underneath. The leather laces of a pair of platform sandals crisscrossed her calves.

And just about finished him.

What the hell was wrong with him? He'd been watching the girls dance for weeks now, first at Rosey's Marietta club, then here. He'd seen them fully dressed, damn near naked and everything in between. It had become so commonplace that he hardly noticed anymore.

So why had he suddenly started noticing Amanda?

Breaks were few and Amanda had always protected every moment of hers. For every hour she'd spent in a college classroom, she'd spent two in this oversize closet, reading, cramming. Everyone knew to leave her alone when she was there. Oh, Eternity dropped in sometimes, always curious about Amanda's studies and her plans for the future.

But the break was slipping away, and there was Rick blocking the door, saying nothing, just looking. *Men have probably always looked at you,* Julia had said. Men, sure. A Calloway? Just once, and she'd paid for that.

But that was a long time ago. She was all grown-up now. Her father was dead, her mother hardly spoke to her and soon she would be starting a new life. Nothing Rick could say or do could hurt her. Life, and her mother and his brother, had made sure of that.

Still, it took courage to turn her back, stroll across a few feet of plush carpet brought from home and seat herself on the chaise. She swung her legs onto the cushion, then picked up her book. "Did you come here for a reason?"

"Yeah. But damned if I can remember what it was." The words were accompanied by a charming grin that could have fluttered every female heart in the place. But her heart wasn't fluttering. It was just indigestion from the too-rich chocolate she'd eaten before his visit.

"Then close the door on your way out, will you?" She opened the book to the dog-ear marking her place and began to read again. At least, she went through the motions. She squinted at the words, getting each one into her brain in order but understanding none of them. She had no problem, though, understanding that he hadn't left the room. That he still stood there, still looked at her. She ignored him as long as she could before lowering the book and asking, "Is there a reason you're still here?"

"Are those your reading glasses?"

She glanced at the wire-framed glasses on the table. "Everything in here is mine."

"So why aren't you wearing them?"

Picking them up, she slid them into place. She wasn't vain. As glasses went, they were flattering, and the fact that they brought hazy words into focus made wearing them a no-brainer. The fact that they made Rick hazy instead was another benefit. Plus, she couldn't deny that somewhere down inside, she felt more serious, more substantive, when she wore them.

Did she want Rick to think there was more to her than a nice body?

"Cute," he said, then slid his hand into his pocket. After pulling out a handful of bills, he counted out three twenties, a ten and a five and folded them neatly in fourths. "For today's lesson."

She took money from men on an almost-daily basis, but not from a Calloway since fifteen summers ago when she had clerked part-time at the Copper Lake Lumberyard, owned by Rick's uncle Garry. He'd paid her in cash, folding the money in exactly the same way, delivering it with an oily smile and a look in his eyes that had made her feel small and insignificant.

At the end of that summer, Robbie had made her feel even worse.

But Rick's look wasn't any different than usual and he'd saved her the trouble of folding the bills herself. Accepting them, she slid them into the thin slot barely noticeable in the platform of her left shoe. Tip-jar shoes, they were called, giving a dancer a secure place to keep her tips when she was onstage…or in a back room.

"Thanks," she said, then lowered her gaze to the book again, expecting him to leave.

He didn't. "Do you think Julia will loosen up enough to actually get on a stage?"

Proust would have to wait for another day, Amanda acknowledged, closing the book and removing her glasses. "I don't know. She says she wants to. A lot of people will do whatever it takes to get what they want."

Like her. She'd worked hard to get what she wanted and she firmly believed the struggle would make the success that much sweeter.

"Do you think you could persuade Harry to give her a shot here?"

"You want to watch her dance in front of strangers?" There was that *ick* feeling she'd experienced earlier in the day.

"I want to keep an eye on her. She's not used to places like this."

"I can ask, depending on how the next lessons go." Amanda had worked with Harry for years and she'd rarely asked favors of him. Because of that, and because she was popular with his customers, he would likely give Julia a shot without sending her to one of the smaller clubs first.

"Does your boyfriend ever come and watch you?"

She glanced at the clock, then stood, balancing on the eight-inch platforms as naturally as on bare feet. "No boyfriend."

"What about the guys you date?"

"None of them, either. I've had priorities," she said as she checked her appearance in the mirror, adjusting the headband. "Save money, buy my house, finish my degree. There will be time to worry about relationships when I retire."

Rick's brows raised. "You plan to wait another thirty or forty years before you look for a guy?"

She turned away from the mirror and replaced his reflection with the real thing. "When I retire from dancing. Five weeks and five days from today."

He still looked surprised. "Then what will you do?"

She couldn't contain the smile that spread from ear to ear. "When the spring semester begins in January, I'll be the newest English lit teacher at the James C. Middleton College of Liberal Arts."

He thumbed in the direction of the main room. "The old guys out there? The budget committee?"

She nodded. "Dean Jaeger, the one who wears the bow ties, was my advisor. When the job opened, he suggested I apply. I did, and they hired me."

"And they don't mind your dancing?"

Any traditional school would have found her background objectionable. Amanda had been prepared for that. She had even considered more than once changing her major—had acknowledged that to get a teaching job *anywhere,* she would have to gloss over her background at best, flat-out lie about it at worst. "They take the *liberal* part of their name seriously. Having a former stripper teach English lit seems perfectly reasonable to them."

"Wow. I never had teachers like you in college. I might have paid more attention if I had."

She hadn't thought about his own college degree. Higher education had been a given for all Calloways, and the University of Georgia had been the place. They went on to successful lives. Amazing what advantages could do for a person. And yet Rick was tending bar in a strip club. How had that happened and how did it sit with the family back in Copper Lake?

The questions were nothing more than mild curiosity, she told herself, and she brushed them aside as easily as she gestured toward the hallway behind him. "Break's over. I've got to go."

He stood there a moment longer, then stepped aside. "Got to go entertain the budget committee," he remarked, an odd note of *something* in his voice.

She didn't try to figure out what it was, but slipped past him and went down the hall. When she turned into the dressing room doorway, he was still standing there. When she came out a moment later, he was gone. Relief seeped into her muscles, though she wasn't about to examine why his presence—or absence—even registered.

As she approached the stage door, a new song started. Pop was the music of choice at Almost Heaven, though on occasion she opted for blues or something Latin, sensual and sexual and steamy. At the moment, even with no sign of Rick, she was happy to have the pop. It would keep things cool.

Keep *her* cool.

The stage lights were bright enough to make the customers shadowy, but there was nothing muted about their reception. There was a whistle or two, some applause, a murmur of encouragement as she wrapped herself around the pole. She used the pole much as a woman might use her lover, swaying around it, rubbing against it, sliding down until her knees were splayed, then rising again, twisting until the pole was centered in her back, repeating the long, languid slide down.

Her eyes were half closed, her lips half curved, as she let the music surround her. Dancing came as naturally to her as breathing. She heard a note or two, and her body began to sway. She didn't have to think, plan or concentrate. The music took over, and everything else faded into the background. The voices, the heat that formed a sheen over her skin, the gazes and leers…none of it mattered. Only the music.

She loosened the chain around her waist, letting its length trickle between her fingers into a small mound at the base of the pole. The hook that secured her dress was next to go. With a shimmy, the gold lamé puddled at her feet, leaving her in a strapless black bra and a thong. The act brought the usual reaction, still muted in her music-dazed brain…then her muscles went taut. A shiver rippled along her skin, making her feel *exposed;* heat followed in its wake.

Opening her eyes, she searched for the gaze that could create such awareness through the haze, knowing before she saw him that it was Rick. He stood off to the side, just inside the door that led to the back hallway, arms crossed over his chest. He looked formidable enough to be a bouncer and drop-dead sexy enough to be any woman's fantasy.

And he was watching her with enough intensity to make her feel like *his* fantasy.

She turned her back to him. He was a Calloway. He worked at the club. He was involved with Julia. More than enough reasons to keep her distance. But that didn't stop the warmth from seeping deeper inside her. It didn't stop her nipples from drawing into hard peaks. It didn't stop the rush of desire that welled in her belly.

She felt like a newbie, experiencing the power of her own sexuality for the first time. Fine for an eighteen-year-old, way past ridiculous for her now. *Focus on the music.* That was how she'd survived her first night—hell, her first month—on the job. How she'd survived twelve years.

It was how she would survive this dance.

After his last customer left, Rick headed straight for the back door. He wanted to be out quickly enough to miss Amanda. After her dance in the goddess outfit, he'd needed another break to get his body temperature somewhere close to normal. Unfortunately, Chad hadn't been willing to extend his time at the bar, so Rick had gone back to work, hot, turned-on and confused.

Sure, she was beautiful, and her body was heart-attack-inducing, but she'd always been beautiful and it had never bothered him before. She hadn't done anything that he hadn't seen a thousand times before, but something—besides his hard-on—had changed. He just couldn't figure out what. Was it because he'd talked to her? He'd been to her house? He'd seen her outside the club, being a normal woman in a normal life?

Maybe it was because he hadn't gotten laid in a while. Undercover operations and women were difficult to manage at the same time, at least for him, so he tended not to mix the two. But he'd been on this job for less than three months. He wasn't so sex-hungry that the first pretty woman could turn him into a horny kid. On this job in particular, he was surrounded by pretty women.

And Amanda was the prettiest of them all. The sexiest. The smartest. The most innocent. The one he hadn't been able to stop thinking about in the past twenty-four hours.

The October night air held a chill that smelled faintly of the Dumpsters at the edge of the parking lot. He took the steps from the stoop to the pavement two at a time and was digging his keys from his pocket when headlights brightened the night. The finely tuned engine of a long white Mercedes broke the quiet as it glided to a stop a few feet in front of Rick.

A scrawny weasel of a guy jumped out of the front passenger seat and hurried around to open the rear door. Leaving his keys in his pocket, Rick watched as Rosey Hines slowly emerged from the car's interior. Beyond the Mercedes—more of a necessity than a luxury, thanks to his bulk—Rosey didn't flaunt his wealth. He wasn't weighted down with gold, he didn't dress flamboyantly and he wasn't attended by a bunch of tough guys meant to intimidate. Rosey was intimidating enough by himself.

"Calloway," he greeted with a nod.

"Mr. Hines."

"How was business tonight?"

"Not bad."

Rosey grinned. "It never is. I do have the best girls in town."

Almost Heaven *was* one of the better clubs, Rick acknowledged. All the dancers were young, pretty and in shape. They didn't need makeup to disguise needle marks or to hide the effects of too much booze; they didn't look as if they lived on the fringes of respectable society. The clientele was better, too—businessmen, professionals. Few blue-collar types ever came through the door. With drinks starting at eighteen bucks and everything else going up from there, they couldn't afford to.

"Is it Chad's turn to lock up?" Rosey asked, and Rick nodded. According to Harry, Rosey knew his employees' work hours better than they did, and he scheduled his visits to the club accordingly. He came only at closing time and only on nights when Chad was working late. That *could* be because Chad was Rosey's cousin once removed, but Rick figured it was more likely because Chad was on Rosey's payroll in more ways than one.

Behind Rick the door opened and soft soles slapped down the first few steps before stopping. Rosey's gaze shifted past Rick and a smile crossed his face. "Amanda."

Of course it was. Rick glanced over his shoulder just long enough to catch a glimpse of a T-shirt, snug jeans and sandals, then switched his gaze back to Rosey.

"Mr. Hines." The footsteps resumed, then Amanda stopped again a few feet to Rick's right.

"Aw, you don't have to be formal around Calloway here," Rosey said with a grin.

Amanda smiled, too. "Hey, Rosey. How's your mother?"

"Enjoying her cruises way too much. She's threatening to spend the rest of her life sailing." Rosey tilted his head Rick's way. "Calloway says the night wasn't bad.

Was it worth coming out or would you have preferred to stay home working on your bedroom?"

What the hell did Rosey know about Amanda's bedroom? And for that matter, how the hell did she know anything about Rosey's mother? He wasn't the type to get too chummy with his employees—only those who had been with him a long time and were involved in his illegal enterprises. Did Amanda fall into that category, or was there something different between them? Either possibility was so repugnant that Rick had to stifle the impulse to step back and put distance between him and both Rosey *and* Amanda.

"—tips will pay for that pricey wallpaper I've been coveting," she was saying when Rick tuned in. "Yeah, it was worth coming out. But it's been a long night. I've got to get off my feet."

"Me, too," Rosey said, setting his girth in motion. "See you. You, too, Calloway."

Rick stepped back to let him pass, followed by the weasel, as Amanda circled the rear of the car. After watching Rosey's slow progress up the first couple steps, Rick headed in the opposite direction, catching up with her about the time she reached her car.

"You're on a first-name basis with the boss?" he asked as she opened the rear door of her car and tossed her bag onto the seat.

Her glance didn't quite reach his face. "I've known Rosey for years. He was the bouncer at the first club I ever worked at."

"And twelve years later he owns five clubs."

"He was always ambitious," she replied with a

shrug, making the glitter-and-paint Eiffel Tower on her shirt ripple.

"You're ambitious, too," he pointed out. "Going from Atlanta's finest strip club to the staff of its most liberal college."

"But because you're not ambitious, that makes it a flaw of some sort in those of us who are?"

Rick rested one hand on the trunk of her car, leaning so his hip was against the rear panel. "What makes you think I'm not ambitious?"

Her whole manner became fluttery—her weight shifting from one foot to the other, her hand making a meaningless little gesture, her gaze sliding away from him, then skittering back again. "You have a college degree, yet you tend bar in a strip club."

"Atlanta's finest strip club," he reminded her. "I said none of my college teachers looked like you. I didn't say I stuck around long enough to graduate."

Though he did. He'd started out in pre-law, like both of his grandfathers, his father, all of his uncles, one of his aunts and, after him, both of his younger brothers. But he'd known from the beginning that he was never going to be a lawyer. Half of the lawyers in the family had never practiced, Granddad Calloway had pointed out. They worked in the family business, protecting what generations before had built, adding on to their success. But they still had the degree. It was family tradition.

Rick hadn't cared enough about tradition to spend the time and money earning a degree he would never use. Over Granddad's protest, he had switched his major to criminal justice and he'd never regretted it.

"So did you graduate?" Amanda asked, toying with her keys.

No. A simple lie. He lied all the time on the job and was pretty damn good at it. He'd better be, since his life depended on it. But for reasons that wouldn't bear close scrutiny, he didn't want to lie at that moment. Instead he asked, "Does it make a difference? Does having a college degree make me smarter, better, more respectable? Does not having one mean I'm not respectable?"

Her gaze held steady for a moment, then the corners of her mouth tilted up. Before she could answer, though, his cell phone gave an annoying buzz. He fished it from his pocket, glanced at the screen, then flipped it open. "Hey, babe."

"There's my first clue that you're not alone," Julia said. "Are you still at the club?"

"I'm just heading out. I'm standing in the parking lot talking to Amanda."

"Tell her hello for me."

He dutifully did so, and Amanda offered her own hello loud enough for the cell phone to pick it up. He pivoted so he was leaning against the car, so Amanda was just a shadow in his peripheral vision instead of dead-on in front of him. "What are you doing up so late?"

"Getting used to the hours. Unpacking. Trying to decide whether to find suitable hiding places around the apartment for my weapons or if I'd just be safer wearing a pistol at all times."

"Aw, it's not that bad." He'd been living there for three months. It wasn't the sort of place Rick Calloway, GBI agent, would choose—his condo was in a much

better part of town—but it was appropriate for Rick
Calloway, bartender. "Listen, babe, I'm heading out.
I'll be home soon."

"Don't surprise me. I might shoot you," Julia muttered.

With a laugh, he hung up, then fixed his attention on
Amanda again. "What were we talking about?" He
didn't need a reminder: she'd been about to tell him that
she was the last person who would judge someone else's
worth by the extent of his education. She'd been about
to smile at him, which would have made him grateful
the car he was leaning against would support his weight
because it would have been questionable whether his
legs could.

It was a good thing Julia had interrupted. A timely
reminder to both him and Amanda that there was
another woman in his life.

"I don't remember, and at the risk of repeating
myself, it's been a long night. I've got to get off my feet.
Tell Julia I'll see her at noon." With a grimace that was
supposed to pass for a smile, she got into her car, started
the engine and drove away.

Rick walked to his own car and, ten minutes later, he
was climbing the stairs to his second-floor apartment.
His boots clanged on the metal tread, with only the thin
light from a nearby streetlamp to light the way. The
bulb next to the door was burned out, broken or stolen
again. He didn't mind the dark—anything he couldn't
take care of himself, the pistol secured to his right calf
could—but for Julia's sake, he should check the bulb.
Not that she would be going out without a pistol, either.

He knocked, then called out, "Hey, Jay, it's me,"

before unlocking the door. He stepped inside, dropping his keys on the table as he closed and locked the door. The jangle of the keys hitting the floor made him turn. And stare.

Ten hours ago he'd left the shabby apartment with its third-rate carpet and fourth-hand furniture. Now rugs covered much of the carpet and throws covered the furniture. The table that had stood next to the door was across the room now. His one measly lamp was gone, replaced by four others that lit up the room like midday, and the musty odor he'd come to associate with the place had been replaced by a fragrant candle scent.

Julia appeared in the hallway that led to two cramped bedrooms and the bathroom. She wore jeans and a T-shirt, with her Sig Sauer holstered on the waistband, but that wasn't what made his eyes widen. He'd seen her in casual clothes before, and wearing a gun, too. But he'd never seen her with her hair thick and loose and curling around her face, or with a real makeup job, or looking pretty.

"Wow."

Color heated her cheeks as she scooped a box from the dining table with jerky movements. "Grab that other box, will you?"

He picked it up, nothing too heavy, and carried it into the bedroom across the hall from his. This room had changed, too. When he'd left for work, it had been an empty room with no sheets on the mattress, no signs of use at all except for the running shoes piled on the floor and the fishing gear laid across the bed. Now those were gone, presumably dumped in his room, and there were more rugs, bedcovers in pale green, tons of pillows, a jewelry case on the dresser, clothes in the closet and shopping bags on the bed.

He set the box on the floor, then picked up one of the shopping bags. "I thought you were just bringing a few things until you passed your audition with Harry."

"This *is* a few things."

"Huh. I moved in three months ago with one suitcase and a box and haven't needed anything else."

"I noticed. You had three bath towels, three washcloths, two coffee cups, a bag of plastic spoons and a jar of instant coffee. No dishes, no dish soap, no sanitizer, no microwave, no books, no television, no stereo, no computer."

"I travel light," he said with a shrug as he looked inside the bag, then removed one of the shoes there. It hardly qualified for the name, with little more than a sole, a clear vinyl strap across the toes and another one that circled the ankle, each topped with a thin pink bow. The heel was slender and long, four or five inches, and could probably substitute as a weapon in the absence of anything else. "You gonna wear these?" he asked cynically, glancing from the heel to the flats neatly lined up on the closet floor.

Julia pulled both the shoe and the bag from his grasp. "I'm going to try."

"What else did you buy?"

She grabbed for the other bag, but he got it first, emptying it on the bed. There was a garment that would have been worthy of the name *shorts* if it had an extra yard of material. A bra and bikini bottom made of silver mesh, with lengths of silver beads dangling from each hip and between the breasts. A navy blue dress, simple, straight, falling just to the hips and with no back. A bra, thong and breakaway skirt in fiery red.

"You gonna wear these?" he asked again, his brows raised to his hairline.

Her jaw tightened as she swept up everything and stuffed it back into the bag. "I'm going to try. Did Hines come by tonight?"

Sobering, Rick leaned against the edge of the dresser. "Yeah, just as I was leaving. Amanda's on a first-name basis with him. Asked him about his mama."

"They've both been in the exotic-dance business a long time." Her nose wrinkled. "Roosevelt Hines and exotic dancing. There's an image that'll be hard to get rid of. You think she could be involved with him?"

No. But Rick kept his gut response inside and considered it rationally. It wouldn't be the first time a woman had slept with her boss. Or the first time a beautiful woman had fallen for an unlikely man. And was Rosey really so unlikely? They were in the same business. He could have been a big help to her career in the past twelve years. He could have given her money, advice, contacts. And she would have given him…a pretty girl on his arm? All the sex the big man could handle?

But Rosey had a criminal record five miles long. Amanda had nothing more than a speeding ticket when she was twenty-two. He was scum who belonged in the underworld where he resided. She'd just been passing through to better things.

Though twelve years was an awfully long time to pass.

"Well?" Julia prodded. "You think Amanda has something going with Hines?"

"You're a woman. What do you think?"

"I think if he came near me, I'd shoot him where it don't grow back."

"But?" With Julia, there was usually a *but*.

She shrugged, her hair shifting in soft waves. "A woman does what she has to. I've never been in Amanda's place. I don't know how she grew up, how she got to where she is today. I don't know what she's had to do."

Rick didn't know any of that about Amanda, either. The background the bureau had done on her was cursory—name, age, address, credit check, criminal record check. It had been sufficient for their purposes.

Now that he'd talked to her, it didn't seem sufficient at all. He wanted to know a whole lot more.

"You know, we're overlooking one possibility," Julia said, clearing everything from the bed, then turning down the covers. The sheets were pastel green and white stripes, and the pillowcases matched, with the addition of tiny roses embroidered in bright pink. "She could actually like the guy."

She could be a nice woman who'd become friends, nothing more, with her sleaze of a boss. Rick would rather think not, but it beat the other possibilities.

He pushed to his feet and went to the door. "Whatever the case, she's leaving the business next month. You've got to be in place well before then."

Julia nodded, her look less apprehensive than it had been before she'd met Amanda. *Do you think she'll loosen up enough to actually get onstage?* he'd asked Amanda.

I don't know, she'd said. *A lot of people will do whatever it takes to get what they want.*

While Julia might not want to strip, she did want to succeed at her job. She would pull it off. For the first time since their boss had suggested it, Rick felt confident of that.

Then he thought again of Rosey and the way he'd smiled at Amanda. What about her? What had she done—what would she do—to get what she wanted?

Chapter 3

Wednesday was one of Amanda's days off. Normally tips were good enough that she worked four days a week, though on occasion she had put in five or six days—when tuition was coming due, when her car needed a new transmission, when her aunt had asked for money for a divorce. Though Amanda hadn't seen Dana in years, she'd given her the cash to pay the lawyer and the deposits on an apartment and utilities.

She hadn't heard from Dana since. But that was all right. Amanda had to live with her conscience, Dana with hers.

"You want to get something to eat?"

Amanda looked at Julia, collapsed on the floor, one foot propped on the stripper's pole. They'd spent the last four hours working, Julia mimicking moves before hesitantly trying a few of her own. She felt foolish, she'd admitted, but Amanda had already figured that out. Every stiff line of her body had screamed it.

But by the end, she'd been a little more relaxed. She'd shown something more than determination—a hint that someday this might come naturally to her.

"Sure," Amanda agreed. She'd had a salad for lunch before Julia had arrived, but that seemed a long time ago.

"I'm supposed to meet Rick at that Mexican place down the block from the club at five-thirty. Is that okay?"

No, Amanda wanted to say. She'd agreed to a meal with Julia. It wasn't fair to throw in Rick after the fact. She didn't want to sit down at a table with him. Didn't want to share a meal. Didn't want to feel that intense gaze on her.

Didn't want to be reminded that he had a thing with Julia.

"Yeah, sure," Amanda said with an awkward smile. "That'll give me time to shower."

Julia sniffed, then her nose wrinkled. "Yeah. Me, too. I'll see you there."

Padding along quietly, Dancer followed them to the door, then trotted into the yard to take care of business. The dog sniffed the flowers, stopped to watch a squirrel in the neighbor's yard, then stopped again to watch Julia drive away.

"Not in any hurry, are you, puppy?" Neither was Amanda. Wasn't it enough that she saw Rick at the club?

But Dancer finally trotted back onto the porch. Amanda opened the screen door for her, then headed for the bathroom herself.

Ninety minutes later, she was showered and shampooed, smelling of exotic spices and looking like any thirty-year-old woman in faded jeans and a lace-edged T-shirt. Her still-damp curls were piled on her head none too tidily and her makeup was her toned-down everyday version. She looked fine for dinner with a friend.

Better than fine for dinner with that friend's boyfriend.

The restaurant was three doors down from Almost Heaven, a mock-adobe hacienda with a red-tile roof and lush vines flowering everywhere. Amanda paused for a moment inside the door to let her eyes adjust to the dimmer light, then the hostess pointed out the corner where Rick waited. Alone.

The table was a half-round booth, barely big enough for three, and he sat with his back to the wall. He wore a white shirt, unbuttoned at the neck, sleeves rolled halfway up his forearms. His fingers were clasped around a practically full glass of beer, his head was tilted back and his eyes appeared to be closed.

"He's a good-looking man," the hostess murmured. "Do you suppose he has a father who's available?"

Amanda shrugged. Gerald Calloway had been dead for as long as she could remember, but according to gossip, before his death he'd *always* been available.

She wove her way between tables and other early diners to the booth. About halfway there, she realized that his eyes had only appeared to be closed. Though he showed no signs of awareness, she felt the instant his gaze locked in on her.

When she slid onto the seat across from him, he raised his head and fully opened his eyes. "Hey."

"Hey." She ordered iced tea from the waiter who'd followed her, then gestured to the empty margarita glass beside him. "Where's Julia?"

"In the bathroom. The margarita didn't sit well on an empty stomach. She was too nervous to eat lunch before going to your house."

Amanda nodded. "She did fine today."

"Good."

That was the extent of their conversation until Julia returned from the ladies' room. She looked paler than usual and the smile she gave them both was sickly. Instead of waiting for Rick to stand up and let her slide into the middle, she bumped against him, pushing him over. He looked as if he wanted to protest—Amanda certainly wanted to—but moved, giving her his seat.

"Oh, man," Julia said, patting her face with her napkin. "No booze ever again. I see why you don't drink."

Since Rick was sipping his beer at that moment, Amanda assumed the comment was directed to her. "I work too hard to stay in shape. If I'm going to splurge, it's going to be on chocolate and ice cream."

Rick gave her a long look—at least, the part of her he could see. "You don't look like you ever splurge." His voice was normal, his comment a simple statement. But it was the look that sent a tiny shiver down her spine, that raised her temperature a degree.

The look, and the fact that his girlfriend was sitting right next to him, oblivious.

Amanda turned her attention to the menu, though she always ordered the same thing. Better than looking at

Rick, though, and feeling that little sexual tingle, or looking at Julia and feeling guilty.

After placing their orders with the waiter, Amanda and Julia chatted about pretty much nothing until the food came. Halfway through the meal, Julia put her fork down, pushed her plate away and fixed her gaze on Amanda. "Would it be okay if I come by the club some night and just watch?"

The memory of Rick "watching" the night before streaked through Amanda, leaving heat and edginess behind. It made her throat tighten, made her hand tremble when she picked up her glass for a sip. "That's what we're there for," she replied with a smile she couldn't hold for more than a moment.

"I think maybe I could learn something. Could I meet some of the other dancers, too?"

"Sure. Anytime you want." Preferably on Rick's night off, though he'd be likely to accompany her. He'd said he wanted to keep an eye on her, hadn't he?

Amanda's father was the first and last man to care about keeping her safe. He'd lost the physical ability to protect her when she was six, but emotionally, he'd been there for her until the day he died. She missed that. Missed having someone who would worry if she didn't come home. Missed having someone to share things with.

She missed having a man in her life.

"Are you friends with all of them?" Julia asked, then smiled deprecatingly. "I know I'm probably totally naive, but I imagine it's like some kind of sisterhood. You know, exotic dancers united against the rest of the world."

Amanda glanced at Rick, leaned back, one arm

resting on the seat cushion at Julia's back, apparently content to listen to the conversation without contributing, then she shrugged. "I'm friendly with all of them, but not necessarily friends. It's like any group of women who work together. Some are nice. Some aren't. Some are competitive. Some are jealous. The younger girls are looking for friends or mentors—or mothers," she added drily, thinking of the eighteen- and nineteen-year-old kids she'd helped along. Even when *she* was nineteen, she'd felt years older.

"How old do you have to be to dance?"

"Eighteen most places."

"How old were you?"

She finished the last of her tea and folded her hands in her lap. "Eighteen."

Julia shook her head. "Wow. I was finishing high school and starting college then. And you—" she elbowed Rick "—were probably raising hell back home at eighteen and making everyone grateful you were leaving for college, too."

"Hey, there were plenty of people who were sorry to see me go," he protested.

"Let me guess. All of them female and under the age of twenty."

"Twenty-two." His gaze narrowed, as if he were thinking hard, then relaxed again. "No, twenty-four."

Julia laughed. Mention of girls in his past didn't seem to faze her at all. She must trust him a lot, Amanda thought, and envied her that. Most of the men in her past had been trustworthy only about as far as she could have thrown them.

"How did you get into dancing?" Julia asked, including Amanda in the conversation again.

"I had a friend who danced. She badgered me into auditioning and…" She shrugged as if to say, Here I am. And it was basically true. Just the shortened version. She had intended the dancing to be a temporary thing, just something that was fun and would give her a little extra cash to make life easy for once. Financially, life *had* gotten easier, practically from the first day. Emotionally, it had taken a nosedive. Her mother and her aunt had both objected strenuously—first to the dancing, then to her. They'd wheedled, coaxed, demanded, judged and damned, and her relationship with them had never recovered.

The waiter began clearing dishes from the table. "Would you like some dessert? Fried ice cream, flan, sopaipillas?"

"Sopaipillas," Rick said. "With three spoons."

Amanda's mouth watered, though she was experienced at resisting temptation. She took a sidelong look at Rick and reminded herself: *very* experienced.

"Great," Julia said grumpily. "And I'm supposed to be watching my weight."

"Your weight's fine," Rick said. His tone was absent-minded and he didn't make any sweet gestures, like squeezing her hand or giving her that amazingly sexy smile. More curious to Amanda, Julia didn't seem to notice either the tone or the lack of gestures.

The woman wanted to strip because she wanted to know how it felt to have men look at her and think she was sexy. She'd been stuffy all her life and wanted to be different, just for a time. She had a drop-dead gorgeous boyfriend whom other women thought was incredibly sexy, but she didn't seem the least bit insecure.

Interesting relationship.

When the waiter returned with the sopaipillas, he set the platter in the center of the table and left three napkin-wrapped spoons. The rectangles of fried dough were drizzled with cinnamon, chocolate and honey, and separated by mounds of soft whipped cream. Rick dug in and so did Julia, after murmuring, "I'm sure I'll regret this...."

But after the first bite, she stiffened and her skin took on a pallid cast. "Oh," she said, injecting a wealth of meaning into the single syllable. "I don't—"

She slid to her feet, one hand pressed to her stomach, and held out her other hand. "Give me my purse, will you? I'm going home before—" A burp interrupted her. Flushing, she grabbed the purse Rick held out and bolted for the door.

"Shouldn't you go with her?" Amanda asked.

There wasn't a shred of concern in Rick's expression. "Do you want someone around when you puke up your guts?" He slid the platter closer to her. "It's got chocolate, and whipped cream is close enough to ice cream."

"But—"

"Julia will be fine. It'll just make her think twice about drinking on an empty stomach. Or eating spicy food when she's just thrown up. Or rich food."

"I'll just check—"

He extended his hand, and Amanda stopped both her words and her movement to stand. "Let her go. She's embarrassed enough. She'll go home, crawl into bed and sleep it off."

Crawl into *his* bed. Sleep it off with him—sooner or later—at her side.

Warmth spread through Amanda. Lust? Envy? Guilt? Since none was better than the other, she preferred not knowing and sank back onto the bench.

"So…" Rick nudged the third spoon closer to her. "Are you and Mr. Hines friends or just friendly?"

She watched as he cut off a chunk of dough, drenching it with sweetness, then lifted the spoon to his mouth. Watched as his lips closed over the gooey good stuff, as his jaw worked when he chewed, and she almost sighed. Not because it was Rick. Not because he made eating sexy. Just because the dessert looked so damned tempting.

Yeah, sure. It was the dessert that tempted her.

Knowing she shouldn't, she picked up the napkin and unwrapped the spoon. She took her time cutting off a small corner of one pastry, took even more time drenching it in the sauces, then slid it into her mouth. This time she did sigh.

He laughed. "That sounded almost obscene. It's good, isn't it?"

She nodded, still savoring the flavors.

"It's okay to indulge once in a while. Go ahead." He edged the plate closer. "Finish it off."

The plate was near enough now that she could smell the warm fragrance of the cinnamon, the distinct sweetness of the honey, the dark richness of the chocolate. She frowned at him. "Are you trying to tempt me?" Almost instantly her cheeks heated. Wrong words, wrong person to say them, definitely wrong person to say them to.

He scooped up a spoonful of the sauces and held it in midair. "Can I tempt you?"

No, no, no. Three strikes. He's out, remember?

She baldly returned to the earlier subject. "Why are you so interested in Rosey?"

He shrugged. "He's the boss, but I really don't know much about him."

"He sees that you're paid on time. What more do you need to know?"

Another shrug, another sexy ripple. "I guess I'm just a curious guy."

"Haven't you heard that curiosity killed the cat?"

Outwardly, nothing changed. He still sat, loose-limbed and relaxed. He still swirled his spoon in the sauce. His gaze was still lazy, even disinterested. But something sharpened the air around him. Something about him seemed *very* interested. "Is that a warning?"

Amanda blinked. Warnings were for vulnerable people, people who might find themselves at a disadvantage in a dangerous situation. She couldn't begin to imagine Rick being vulnerable, no matter what. "No. It's an old saying. That's all."

"I've heard that not all of his business interests are legal."

Indulgence over, she put down her spoon, then folded her arms across her middle. "Almost Heaven is, and that's the only one I care about." Then, unable to resist, she asked, "Are you looking to get cut in on the ones that aren't?"

He gave a good impression of actually considering it before he grinned. "Nah. It would break my mama's heart."

"*You* have a mother?" she scoffed even as a picture of Sara Calloway came to mind—pretty, blond, always the image of the genteel Southern lady. Amanda's mother had waited on Sara at the restaurant, at the shop, and had been unrelentingly jealous of her. *Life always goes her way,* Brenda had fumed more than once. *She's got everything.*

And Brenda had had nothing but a husband who needed twenty-four-hour care and a daughter who was last on her list of priorities. She blamed the Calloways for David's accident, for the two and sometimes three jobs she worked, for the drudgery of everyday life and the lack of a future.

Fifteen years had passed since David's death, fifteen years since Amanda and her mother had moved to Atlanta, and not a lot had changed. Brenda now worked one job; she didn't have an invalid husband to care for or a daughter to neglect. But life still wasn't what she wanted.

"My mother's a very nice woman," Rick said, pulling her out of her thoughts. "You'd like her."

"I like mothers fine, but they usually have a problem with me."

"Mom wouldn't."

Maybe not. Unlike the other Calloway women, Sara had always been friendly to the working class in Copper Lake. She hadn't treated them like servants too stupid and common to associate with. But being nice to people who worked in her family business and contributed to her family fortune was one thing. Being nice to a stripper who was attracted to her eldest son was another entirely.

"Does she know you tend bar in a strip club?"

"She knows I tend bar." Both on the job and off, Rick's policy was to stick to the truth as much as possible. The fewer lies he told, the fewer chances he would get caught in them. So Sara knew he was working in a bar, but she also knew it was part of his job. She didn't like it when he was undercover. It gave him reason, she claimed, to forget all those lessons she'd taught him and his brothers about right and wrong.

He hadn't forgotten anything, and in her heart Sara knew it. It was just her way of covering how much she worried about him.

"What about your mom?" he asked. "Does she know you dance in a strip club?"

"She does. And she doesn't approve. We don't speak often—Christmas. Her birthday. Mother's Day."

She didn't mention her own birthday. So Mom didn't approve of her daughter's job, but Amanda made an effort anyway. No matter what he or his brothers did for a living, Sara would never shut them out of her life.

"Does she live around here?"

Amanda nodded. "Does yours?"

"No. She still lives in the town where I grew up— the town where *she* grew up. A little place no one's ever heard of."

Amanda's smile was soft. Young. "The same place half the people in Atlanta are from, including me. I'll never go back."

Rick shrugged. He didn't have any bad memories of

Copper Lake, other than his father, but he couldn't see himself ever moving home again. Maybe if he got married and had kids and wanted someplace small and safe for them to grow up…

Not that he'd ever been tempted by the idea of marriage or kids.

"My brothers have stayed there. Russ is in construction and Robbie's a lawyer."

Something flickered across her face, there and gone so fast he couldn't identify it. Surprise that he really did have a family? Horror that there were two more just like him out there? He could have reassured her. Russ was quiet, dependable and responsible, and Robbie was…well, none of those things. In fact, in spite of being a lawyer, he was the least respectable of the bunch.

"I have no brothers," Amanda volunteered. "No sisters, either."

"Just the sisterhood of strippers," he said with a grin.

Her smile was faint, barely formed. "I've been close to some. I tend to attract the new girls, the really young ones who need advice. Some of them are *so* young. They're just not prepared for life in the real world."

"You said dancers have to be eighteen in most places."

"But eighteen can be much younger for some kids than it is for others."

He knew that was true. Hell, Robbie was thirty, same as Amanda, but outside of work, he acted about ten years younger. Maturity wasn't one of his strengths.

He shifted on the bench, turning to face her more, aiming for a totally casual attitude. "I met a girl at the

Marietta club named Tasha. She looked about fifteen—acted that young, too. Do you know her?"

"Blond hair, big brown eyes?"

He nodded.

"That's Tasha Wiley. She danced at Almost Heaven for a while. And she was nineteen."

"Where did she go?"

Amanda shrugged. "She said she got a better offer. That usually means dancing at someone else's club, finding a man with plenty of money that he wants to spend on you or maybe even finding a guy who's willing to overlook your past and marry you." She gazed down for a moment, then, her tone subdued, went on. "It can also mean taking a job filming adult movies or working the streets. Rosey doesn't tolerate his dancers using drugs. It's not good for business. The girls who start using leave to work elsewhere."

"I wouldn't have pegged Tasha for a junkie."

"No, me, neither. I suspect her better offer had to do with a man. She may come back someday or she might live happily-ever-after in Buckhead."

The image of Tasha living in one of Atlanta's better neighborhoods didn't amuse Rick. He also suspected her disappearance had to do with a man—Rosey. Unlike Amanda, though, he doubted she would ever be seen again.

"Does it happen often?" he asked, and Amanda raised her brows in response. "The better offer. Legitimate ones."

"Sometimes. I know a number of dancers who have retired and are married, raising kids, driving a minivan and going to church on Sunday."

"Their husbands know and don't care?"

"Some. The others don't know and hopefully never will."

"Would you lie about it?"

"Not to the man I was going to marry."

"But you would lie to others?"

She shrugged and one curl slipped loose from the mass on her head. It swung, brushing her cheek, before she pushed it behind her ear. "Stripping doesn't make me any less qualified to teach English lit. It doesn't make me any more likely to lead the students astray. It doesn't mean I'll advocate any particular lifestyle or career path. But it's highly doubtful that any school other than Middleton would have hired me knowing how I spent the last twelve years. If Middleton hadn't offered me a job, would I have lied about my background to get a teaching job someplace else? Probably. Yeah, I would have."

At least she was honest about her dishonesty. He appreciated that. Still, he pointed out, "That's not fair."

"Haven't you learned? Life isn't fair." She glanced at her watch, then reached for the ticket the waiter had brought with dessert.

Rick grabbed it first. "I'll pay."

"No, thanks. You didn't invite me—"

"But I enjoyed it."

She held his gaze, her hazel eyes narrowed, her lips flattened. Then, less than graciously, she said, "Thanks. I'll take care of the tip."

She left a generous tip on the table, stood and started toward the door. He followed, his gaze on the sway of her hips. Her jeans fit like a second skin, topping out two inches below her waist; the wide lace hem of her shirt stopped an inch or two above that. The skin revealed there was pale gold, enticing. If he walked beside her, he could put his hand in the small of her back, could let his fingers graze across that skin and see if it was as soft as it looked. It would be warm and his touch there would send a shiver through her. Just a touch would make him hot and hard and—

Realizing she'd stopped moving, he did, as well, just in time to avoid plowing over her. They'd reached the cash register next to the door and he hadn't even noticed. Stepping past her, he gave the check and three twenties to the cashier, pocketed his change, then opened the door for Amanda.

Outside, she faced him. "Thanks for dinner."

"Consider it a trade."

A breeze blew that curl against her cheek again and she absently brushed it away again. "For what?"

"I need a ride home. Julia and I came together. I'm without a car."

She looked as if she wanted to refuse, but gestured toward her car instead. It was a lot like Julia's car—not bad if transportation was all you wanted. It wouldn't win any races or any points for appearance, but it was clean, comfortable and the engine turned over on the first try.

"What do you usually do on your nights off?" he asked, settling into the seat.

She looked both ways before pulling out of the parking lot in the direction he indicated. "Read. Watch TV. Work on my house."

Rosey had said something about working on her bedroom the night before, and the idea that he'd known anything about her bedroom had surprised—annoyed?—Rick. It hadn't occurred to him when he'd chosen to approach her regarding Julia that she might be friends with the boss. Even with Julia's rational explanation, Rick still found it creepy.

"Your house looks fine," he said. "What is there to do?"

Signaling, she checked the rearview mirror, then looked over her shoulder before changing lanes. Then she smiled. "You haven't seen my bedroom."

Simple smile, innocent words, and they had the effect of a punch in the gut. He would like to see her bedroom. Would like to see her in it. Not wearing her stripper clothes, but her this-is-who-I-am stuff. Tight jeans, lace tops, T-shirts, everyday lingerie. Nothing at all.

But he was undercover. Worse, he was undercover as Julia's live-in boyfriend. Worse yet, Amanda was a subject in an investigation. Depending on what was between her and Rosey, she could even wind up being one of the targets of the investigation. There was no way he could risk getting involved with her.

But there was nothing wrong with tempting himself a little, was there? He was strong. When it was time to make a decision, he always made the right one.

"What's wrong with your bedroom?" he asked, indicating that she should turn right at the next intersection. Again with the turn signal, the mirror checks and over-the-shoulder looks. She was a cautious driver.

Who worked as a stripper.

For Rosey Hines.

"My house was built in 1934. All the mechanical stuff was updated over the years, but it still had the original paint and wallpaper when I moved in. I've redone every room except the bedroom, and I'm working on it now."

"So you're good with your hands." His gaze automatically shifted to her hands, loosely gripping the steering wheel at ten and two, just as he'd been taught years ago in driver's ed. They were small, capable, her fingers long and slender, her nails painted some dark shade that was probably called crimson or scarlet but was really just red. She wore rings on four fingers; the shadow of a fading bruise darkened one knuckle. "And you're coveting some fancy wallpaper."

She stopped at a red light and gave him a steady look. "My house is to me what your car is to you."

That was putting it in terms he understood. She could have bought a newer house, that needed less work, that was a cookie-cutter copy of a million other houses out there, just as he could have bought the latest-model car. But where was the fun in that?

"Those are the apartments," he said, gesturing to the complex ahead on the right. "Turn in this entrance and go all the way around to the back." Then he added, "I'm flattered you noticed the car."

Her cheeks turned pink, but he went on. "She's supposed to attract notice. That's part of what I've spent so much time and money on."

"She?"

He grinned. "I think all sleek, powerful, beautiful things are female." Including her. Sleek? Oh, yeah, when she moved on the stage like a predatory jungle cat, sinuous and fluid. Powerful? She turned intelligent men into tongue-tied idiots. And beautiful…oh, hell, yeah.

She slowed to the posted speed of ten miles per hour, a rarity in this parking lot. For once he was glad it was a sprawling complex and that his apartment was at the rear, where it overlooked the parking lot and Dumpster alley.

"Do you come by your remodeling skills naturally?"

She scoffed. "I wish. Trial and error, with a huge debt of thanks to the home improvement center. I'm on a first-name basis with all the guys down there. I started out of ignorance. I had no clue what I was in for. Then, when I found out, it became a challenge to finish. Now I'm pretty good at it. If I hadn't gotten the teaching job at Middleton, I could have gone into business painting, plastering and tiling."

"You could've given new meaning to 'stripping paint.'"

She smiled again, that simple sucker-punch smile, as she pulled into the parking space next to his car. She shifted into Reverse, making clear she wasn't staying long, then gazed at the building, where lights shone in every apartment. "I hope Julia's feeling better."

He looked, too. His living room lights were on, but his bedroom was dark, and her room was out of sight on the other side of the apartment. "I'm sure she is."

"How long have you two been together?"

He stuck to the truth. "Three years, give or take." That was when they'd both transferred onto the Organized Crime squad and had worked their first case together. Besides being the truth, more or less, that amount of time would explain why they weren't overly affectionate in public. A lot of months together, a lot of time to get over the initial lust and start taking each other for granted. Time enough for their sex life to need a little spicing up.

"After three years together, you should marry her."

His laughter was spontaneous, as much shock as humor. He could see himself married someday, but to Julia? She was his partner, a friend of sorts, as comfortable to be around as one of his female cousins or his mother. While there were men who found her just their type, he wasn't one of them, and he had no doubt she felt the same about him.

"How long have you been alone?" he countered.

Amanda shrugged delicately.

"You should find a man." The thought created a small knot of distaste in his gut. He opened the car door, the overhead light throwing both light and shadows across her face, and climbed out, then bent so he could see her again. "Let's make a deal. You worry about your love life and I'll worry about mine."

She shrugged again in agreement. "Thanks for dinner."

"Thanks for the ride." He pressed the button to lock the doors, closed the door, then stepped out of the way as she backed out of the space. A moment later the taillights of her car disappeared, ten miles per hour, around the next building, but he still stood there. Watched. Waited for his common sense to return. Wondered if it would come back in time to make this case easier.

Then movement upstairs caught his attention, and he saw Julia standing at the living room window, also watching and waiting.

Nah, the case couldn't be too easy. Interesting cases never were. Amanda Nelson was just a complication, and he'd learned over the years how to handle complications. He would handle her.

Just not the way he'd like to.

It rained Thursday morning, not a downpour, but one of those steady showers that seemed to create themselves out of the ever-present humidity. No winds, no threat of lightning or thunder, just gray clouds and a nice steady shower that would be over in an hour, two at most.

Amanda liked running even in storms and she had a dozen regular routes to choose from. This morning she'd chosen the least used of them all. The trek led her through neighborhoods much like her own and around apartment complexes similar to Rick's—big, sprawling, dreary. She had lived in a place just like that when she'd started dancing. For someone like Rick, whose biggest concerns were a bed to sleep in and someone to sleep there with him, it probably seemed fine, even though he could afford a better place on what Rosey paid and the tips the dancers all shared with him.

For Julia, though…she was too fastidious to want to live in such a place. But she did it for Rick, because she loved him. Logical? Yes. Even though she didn't act like a woman in love. All through dinner the night before, they'd shared no little touches, no secret looks, no private smiles. They'd seemed like friends, and not of the intimate nature.

But Julia was uptight. Maybe she had rules for conducting relationships. Maybe they were politely friendly in public and they saved all that intimacy and passion for private. Maybe Rick had doted on her after dinner, had babied her and held her until she'd felt better. Maybe she'd already been feeling better and they'd jumped each other's bones through the rest of the night.

She thought too much about Rick and Julia. Nothing had changed. Rick worked at the club. He was Julia's boyfriend. He was Robbie's brother. He was the wrong person to lust after in so many ways that it wasn't funny.

She was nearing the midpoint of her run, the whole reason she'd mapped out this particular route. It was a small white duplex, surrounded by other small white duplexes. The porch on the left held two patio chairs and potted flowers on its porch; the other porch was bare. The yard on the left was neatly mowed and beds of flowers edged it all the way to the sidewalk. The right yard was overgrown and choked by clumps of dead grass. The porch on the left held chimes and a flag in autumn hues. The right held a faded sign that said No Solicitors.

Amanda slowed as she crossed the street, then walked along the sidewalk, switching off the music on her iPod when she stopped. She'd never been inside the duplex on the right. An invitation would mean the world to her, and it might come in the near future. Once she'd left Almost Heaven, once she was settled into the new job and could prove that she was respectable.

Which wouldn't change the fact that for twelve years, her mother had been ashamed of her. What kind of relationship could they build out of that?

The sound of pounding footsteps caught her attention

and she turned to watch a tall, lean figure approaching. He wore shorts and nothing else, a fact that thudded into her brain with each jarring step. Dark hair, slicked back from his face. Broad chest, dusted with hair. Muscular arms, long legs, thighs and calves knotted with muscle. A nice toasty brown all over that would have been enticingly sweaty if not for the rain. She was surprised he didn't have a trail of female drivers following him just to enjoy the view.

She was more surprised to see him here, on *her* route. "You followed me," she accused when Rick came close enough.

He carried his T-shirt in one hand, wrapped around a bottle of water. After taking a long drink, he looked her in the eye. "Yeah."

"Why?"

"Consider yourself inspiration."

Plenty of men—customers, joggers and others—had told her over the years that her legs and butt were her best features. They should be. She worked damn hard on them. "So you're a bartender, on occasion you fill in for Chad at the door, you're a curious guy and you're a stalker."

He grinned. "Aw, I'm not stalking. It's the middle of the day. I called your name twice, but you didn't hear or you just ignored me." Reaching out, he tugged one of the ear buds for her iPod. "Don't you know it's dangerous to run with music in your ears? It blocks out other noises like traffic and real stalkers."

"I keep the music low enough to hear a car horn or a siren."

"Yeah, well, real stalkers don't generally announce themselves with horns or sirens."

She started walking again and he kept pace.

"Truth is, I usually run on Calhoun. Lot of traffic, distractions, pollution. I saw you turning onto a side street and I figured you'd have a better route worked out. So I followed you."

Once they'd crossed the street again, she eased into a slow jog. "So I'm not the traffic/distractions/pollution sort."

"Oh, you're great at distractions. What's with the house?"

She glanced over her shoulder just before the gentle curve of the street blocked the view. "It's just a house. A turnaround point. From my house to there and back again is exactly four-point-three miles."

"And you like to run four-point-three miles every day?"

"No. I usually run three miles."

"So Thursday's the exception, when you increase your distance by forty-some percent."

She clamped her mouth shut, then changed the subject. "How is Julia?"

He looked ahead instead of at her. "Fine. She had a yoga DVD on when I left."

"She's taking up yoga?" Amanda was pleased. The slow, controlled movements would help Julia loosen up and become more comfortable with her body.

"Not exactly," Rick replied. "It was on. She was watching it, not doing it. She's pretty convinced her body wasn't made to move that way."

"Did you persuade her otherwise?"

"How the hell—"

Amanda caught his grimace, quickly wiped away as he stopped himself. *How the hell would I know?* Was that what he'd been about to say? Having sex with her for three years should have given him a good idea of exactly what she was capable of.

Theirs was one very strange relationship. And it was none of Amanda's business.

A block or so passed in silence before he spoke again. "That girl we were talking about last night—Tasha. Do you know any way to get in touch with her?"

"Isn't she a bit young for you?"

He looked affronted, but said nothing in his defense.

A strange relationship indeed. She shook her head, her curls dripping rain water down her cheeks. "We weren't close. She wasn't interested in advice."

"Was she close to any of the other girls?"

"Just one—DinaBeth." She smiled faintly at the image of the redhead from Peach Orchard, Georgia. Her real name was Diana Elizabeth, but DinaBeth, she'd decided, made for a better stage name. She'd even dotted the *i* with a star, for the fame she was sure to find someday. Like too many dancers, she'd been cut out of her family's lives, but after the initial hurt, her motto had been Screw 'em. She was better off without them, she'd insisted.

Sadly, it might have been truth rather than bravado.

"I haven't seen a DinaBeth at the club," Rick said.

"She quit a few weeks before Tasha."

"Where did she go?"

"I don't know. She got a better offer, too."

"Isn't that unusual?"

The muscles in Amanda's calves were tight and her lungs were starting to protest. With a glance around, she determined she'd already put in her usual three miles. It wouldn't hurt to walk the rest of the way. She slowed, removed the clip that held her hair, squeezed out the water, then fixed it more securely on top of her head.

"Not really," she said at last. "You don't generally get a long-term career in this business. If the looks don't give out, the body does. And a lot of girls never intend to stay long. They earn some fast money and if something better comes along, they grab it."

"Was that what you intended? To earn some fast money, then do something else?"

She studied his expression. There was no judgment there, no condemnation, just simple friendly curiosity. He wasn't interested in the morality of stripping—or strippers. He was asking about her.

"The money was a lure," she admitted. "We never had much of it, and after my father's accident…" It had happened twenty-four years ago this month, on a gray, rainy day like today. She had gone to school that morning, everything right in her world, and had gone home to find out it had all changed.

"What happened?" Rick's voice was quiet, his tone more than just curious.

She rarely talked about that day, or its lasting results, to anyone. Oh, she mentioned that her father had died as the result of an accident, but she'd never acknowledged the long, difficult years between the accident and his death.

"A truck lost its load," she said, stopping for a red light, watching the left-turning traffic pass a few feet away. "He was in the vehicle behind it. His spine was severed, and he suffered some brain damage."

"How old were you?"

"Six when it happened. Fifteen when he died." Nine years of watching the sparkle fade from her dad's life— of watching it fade from her own life. Nine years for Brenda of working two or three minimum-wage jobs, trying to make ends meet, trying to keep some sort of sparkle in her own life.

Rick touched her shoulder; she realized the traffic had passed and the walk sign was flashing. Shaking off the longing for her dad, she crossed the street, matching her pace to Rick's.

"Sorry," he said, sounding sincere. "My father died when I was eleven. Heart attack."

"I'm sorry." She was sincere, too. Her dad had been the best part of her life. She still missed him, still wished she could hear his voice, feel his arms around her, dance with him.

"Don't be. I'm not," Rick said with a careless shrug. His expression, with his skin damp and his dark hair slicked back by the rain, was careless to match. Catching her gaze, he raised his brows and his mouth quirked. "Hell, I would've bet he didn't even have a heart."

Chapter 4

Rick had to give Amanda credit. Her jaw didn't hit the ground and she didn't look at him as if he'd grown a second head or admonish him for saying something so cold. She just kept giving that steady, serious look, pretty much empty of emotion, except for a hint of sympathy. He didn't want it. He was long since over the disappointment Gerald had been.

"What about you?" he asked, directing the conversation back to its original subject. "Have you gotten any better offers?"

She peeled off the bright pink jacket and tied the sleeves around her waist. The jacket had been useless as far as keeping her dry underneath. Her white tank top was plastered to her skin, so damn near transparent that he could see the blue logo on her sports bra. The shirt molded to her breasts, then skimmed across her flat middle, where her thin nylon shorts clung to her hips.

He'd called her a distraction, and it was an accurate description. Just looking at her and watching her move damn near short-circuited his brain. It made him forget that he'd seen her practically naked at the club on more occasions than he could count. This was different. This was sexier.

"I've had offers," she replied, "though, obviously, I didn't think they were better or I would have accepted them."

"Marriage proposals?"

"No. A dozen chances to trade my virtue for an apartment, a car and a monthly allowance. A trip to Europe. A chance to star in *Amanda Does Atlanta.* Job offers in New Orleans, Las Vegas and Hong Kong." She laughed. "But not a soul who wanted to take me home to meet his mother."

Practically cross-eyed at the idea of Amanda doing Atlanta—of Amanda doing *him*—he stumbled over a broken section of sidewalk. Alongside the lust, though, was disgust for the men who'd thought she should sell herself out for an apartment, a car or a trip to Europe. If they'd met her anyplace besides a strip club, they would have shown her more respect.

Or maybe not. Gerald hadn't met any of his girlfriends in strip clubs, and he'd had no more respect for them than he had for his wife. All he'd cared about was himself.

"Once you start teaching, that'll change. I bet all your male students fall in love with you before the semester's over."

She laughed again, this time without the sarcasm that had colored it earlier. "I hope they're too absorbed in the subject matter to even notice the color of my hair."

It wasn't the color of her hair that would absorb them—though he had to admit the long coppery curls had caught his attention the first time he'd seen her. Her back had been to him, and, strange as it seemed, he'd become accustomed to seeing lots of skin, long naked spines, shapely asses and legs that went on forever. But the curls had made her stand out.

"You're teaching lit. *No one's* going to be so absorbed in it that they don't notice everything about you."

"Gee, thanks. You're doing wonders for my confidence." As the rain slacked off, she stopped, then gestured. "This is where I turn."

Looking around, he saw that it *was* her street. That was the quickest two-plus miles he'd done in a long time. "Thanks for the company."

She turned, walking backward along the sidewalk. "Tell Julia hello."

"Julia…yeah."

"Though I'll see her later today myself." With a wave, she turned and picked up her pace to a slow jog.

He watched a moment—pure inspiration—then did the same, heading toward the apartment. As he turned into the complex, the rain grew heavy again. The usual clusters of punks in their teens and early twenties—unemployed, some tough guys, some wannabes—were absent, thanks to the showers. In fact, Rick didn't see another person until he walked into the apartment and found Julia in the kitchen, nuking a cup of instant coffee.

She looked at him, wet and still carrying his shirt, and her nose wrinkled. "You're soaked."

"That's what happens when you go out in the rain without an umbrella or a raincoat." She had brought a trench coat, a slicker and three umbrellas with her. He didn't own any of the above. "Write this down, will you?"

Naturally she didn't have to scramble for something to write with or on. She picked up the ink pen—hers—that rested on the note pad on the counter—also hers—and wrote the address he'd memorized when he'd first encountered Amanda. He hadn't believed for a second that the house was just a convenient turnaround point. It had significance to Amanda and he wanted to know what.

He wanted to know everything about her.

"Give me a minute," Julia said, setting her coffee down and easing past him to get to the computer on the dining table. "You're dripping on the floor."

While she logged on to the Internet, he went into the bathroom, stripped, took a quick shower, then toweled off. As soon as he'd pulled on jeans and a T-shirt, he returned to the living room. "Well?"

"The house belongs to a woman by the name of Roxy Martinez. She has about fifty rental houses all over Atlanta. It's currently rented to Brenda Nelson, who works as an assistant manager at a place called McKettrick's. Pricey clothes, expensive cosmetics, five-hundred-dollars-a-pair shoes. And—" it was apparent by her manner that Julia knew the next was unnecessary, but she confirmed it anyway "—she's Amanda's mother."

The mother who didn't approve of her daughter's occupation, who ignored Amanda's efforts to maintain some sort of contact, lived little more than two miles away. Did she know Amanda sometimes went by her house? Did she ever see her? Talk to her? Invite her in?

Probably not. He figured Amanda planned those runs for when her mother was at work. Less chance of rejection that way.

What had Brenda Nelson's dreams been for her daughter? College, a career? Marriage and motherhood? An easier life than her own had been? Was her disappointment so great that she'd rather not have any contact at all with Amanda?

He made a mental note to touch base with his own mother. His father may not have been worth the air he breathed, but his mom was the best. He should tell her more often.

"Did you find out anything helpful?" Julia asked.

He knew that Amanda was more gorgeous without makeup and drenched to the skin than other women were at their best. That jogging—rather, watching her jog—could be as much foreplay as any other activity. That her father was dead and that, no matter how casual she acted, she missed her mother. That her life growing up hadn't been easy.

But Julia wouldn't share his interest in any of that.

"Tasha's best friend at the club was DinaBeth Jones, who left Almost Heaven for a better offer a few weeks before Tasha's better offer came in."

"Which we already knew."

He didn't object to her pointing out the obvious. She knew as well as he did that neither of them could ask too many questions of Amanda or anyone else at the club without rousing suspicion. Besides, that was the purpose of bringing Julia undercover, so she could ask the questions about the girls.

"She doesn't seem to think there's anything unusual about Tasha and DinaBeth leaving so close together. If something better comes along, you grab it."

"So why is she still doing this after twelve years? I can't believe nothing better's come along."

"She's made her own something better," Rick said absently. "She's quitting in less than six weeks. She already has a teaching job lined up at Middleton."

"Good."

Yeah, he thought so, too.

Leaving the computer, Julia reached across the counter to pick up her coffee, probably not even lukewarm now, and took a sip. "How am I going to bring up the missing girls without making anyone suspicious?"

He held up one finger to signal *wait,* then went into his room. When he returned, he laid a photograph on the table between them. "Tasha, DinaBeth and Lisa." He pointed to each woman in turn. They wore bras, thongs and high, high heels, and were posed arm in arm in front of the bar at Almost Heaven. The shot was fairly well-lit, indicating it had been taken before opening or after closing. The club never saw so much light during business hours. "Lisa Howard sent this to her sister a couple weeks before she disappeared. You can 'find' it in a locker, on the floor, wherever, and ask about them."

Julia nodded, gazed at the three smiling women for a moment, then gravely asked, "What do you think happened to them?"

They could have been killed, forced into working for someone to whom Rosey owed a debt or even sold into some sort of sex-ring operation. They could have been coerced into prostitution or could have been given the starring roles in a series of snuff films.

Or they could be living the good life. There really could have been a better offer.

But Lisa's sister, down in Savannah, was absolutely convinced that Lisa would have stayed in touch with her, no matter what. Unlike DinaBeth and her family, Tasha and hers—Amanda and hers—Lisa hadn't been disowned, criticized or even scolded for her decision to dance. It was just her and her sister, and while her sister hadn't liked Lisa's decision, she hadn't banished Lisa from her life. They'd talked on the phone a couple times a week and e-mailed each other daily.

Until, without warning, the contact had ended. Lisa had quit her job and moved out of her apartment without notice. Her belongings were gone.

Lora Howard knew in her heart that something terrible had happened to her sister.

Rick tended to agree with her.

"I don't know," he replied at last. "You want to hope for the best."

"But be prepared for the worst. Do you think the other dancers at the club are in danger?" More quietly, she asked the question that was really on her mind. "Do you think Amanda's in danger?"

The possibility made Rick's gut clench. Wouldn't that be hell if, just weeks before reaching the goal she'd worked hard for, she vanished without a trace? "I don't know. Probably not. She's friendly with Rosey Hines. She's been around a long time. People would miss her if she disappeared. Besides, these girls are eighteen, nineteen and twenty. Amanda's almost thirty-one."

"Makes me grateful I'm thirty-three." Julia gazed at the photograph again before lifting her gaze. "What if another girl disappears before we find out what's going on?"

Rick didn't answer. It wasn't as if warning the dancers was an option. All they could do was concentrate on their job and hope it didn't get more complicated before it was over.

Hope he didn't fall for Amanda.

Hope he didn't do something unprofessional or dangerous or just plain stupid. He was a guy. Guys were known for being stupid. Sometimes they got lucky and everything turned out all right, like with his brother. A special agent with the Mississippi Bureau of Investigation, Mitch had fallen in love with a subject in his last undercover investigation, and he and Jessica were now playing house in Jackson and planning a Christmas wedding.

But Mitch had had the advantage of knowing that handcuffs with Jessica would be only for fun. The possibility of Rick arresting Amanda was a real one. If she was involved in Rosey's extracurricular activities, if she had any idea what had really happened to the missing girls…

Rick's instincts said she was innocent and he usually trusted them one hundred percent. But this time his instincts wanted to get closer to the subject—wanted to play out their own version of *Amanda Does Atlanta*. This time he couldn't trust them, not completely.

"We live with it," Julia murmured in answer to her

own question. If another girl went missing on their watch, they regretted it. They dealt with it.

And they damn well punished the people responsible.

Loosen up a little tonight, Amanda had told Julia after their afternoon lesson. *Dress casually—jeans, shirt. Nothing too prim.* She'd wanted Julia to be someone the other dancers could relate to when they met for the first time.

Well, she'd worn jeans. Indigo blue. Pressed, with a razor-sharp crease. Flats, navy blue with matching socks. A button-front blouse with about a dozen too many buttons done up. On the upside, her hair was softly curled and her makeup was closer to the makeover Amanda had given her than the very light touch she preferred.

On the downside, she looked prim. Nervous. The respectable, reserved bookkeeper was intimidated by the prospect of meeting a bunch of exotic dancers. "This is about as casual as I get," she said with an apologetic shrug as she met Amanda in the back parking lot of Almost Heaven.

"It's okay," Amanda said. "Buttons can be sexy. Especially if you undo three or four of them."

"I don't suppose it could be three or four at the bottom."

Resting her duffel on the bottom step, Amanda undid the top buttons until a hint of cleavage showed, then opened one more for good measure. She also unfastened the bottom couple buttons, then adjusted the collar. "There. Don't be nervous."

"Easy for you to say," Julia retorted as she followed

Amanda up the steps and into the corridor. "You're not about to walk into a room filled with beautiful, sexy young women who will make you feel dowdy and old."

She was right there. Even when Amanda was eighty-five, white-haired and frail, she had no intention of being dowdy.

"Rick doesn't have any complaints, does he?" Amanda's words were a reminder to herself as well as Julia. Whatever attraction she felt for Rick was out of line. He was taken, and by a woman she'd like to consider a friend. "He loves you the way you are."

A sharp laugh escaped Julia, totally involuntary, as if she found the idea outrageous. It was the same kind of laugh Rick had given the night before when Amanda had suggested that after three years, he and Julia should consider marriage. That was right before he'd told her to mind her own business.

If they weren't in love, why were they together? Great sex? The ease of familiarity? Habit?

Amanda would never settle for any of those. If she was going to be with a man that long, they would be madly in love, like her parents. She wanted that kind of passion and commitment. She wanted to wake up next to a man, knowing that her life was better because he was in it. She wanted to miss him during the day and know that he missed her, too. She wanted to be grateful for each day they were together, wanted to know that they had an *always* together.

She'd rather be alone than find herself spending year after year with a man who wasn't her passion, but was merely okay until someone better came along. She was living proof of that, wasn't she? Soon to be thirty-one and never been in love. Never even really interested…until lately.

Noise filtered through the dressing room's open door as they approached. It would be controlled chaos inside—women dressing, touching up makeup, fixing hair. While some of them were unpleasant and sharp-tongued and a couple were just mean, Amanda was counting on the naturally friendly nature of others to put Julia at ease.

Tossing her bag onto a chair, she introduced Julia around the room. Julia exchanged nods, murmured hellos, then said in an awed tone, "You're beautiful."

Eternity, the subject of her stare, laughed and patted the empty seat beside her. "Come over here, child. I like this one. She has a good eye. Are you a dancer?"

"No. But I'm flattered you asked."

Smiling faintly, Amanda unzipped her duffel. In addition to the usual items—outfits, heels, makeup—she always packed a book or two for her break. This time there was the Proust that Rick had interrupted, along with the latest bestselling thriller. She wasn't sure she would ever be able to read Proust again without thinking about Rick and his charming grin.

She removed her outfit for the first set, then stuffed the bag into her locker. Eternity was chatting up Julia, with a couple of the other girls joining in. "So you're a friend of Amanda's," Eternity said after a few moments.

Amanda caught the reflection of Julia's glance her way in one of the mirrors that lined the wall. "Yes. She's teaching me to dance."

"She's the best," Monique said, getting a few murmurs of agreement along with a few disgruntled snorts.

Julia smiled. "That's what Rick said."

The mere mention of his name caught everyone's attention, including Amanda's. Had he really said she was the best dancer at Almost Heaven? Had he actually watched her enough to have an opinion?

"Rick?" one girl echoed. "The bartending hunk? How do you know him?"

Julia's cheeks turned pink as she stumbled over an answer. "I— He's—"

"She's Rick's girl," Amanda said. It was an old-fashioned term, but one she liked. Her dad had always introduced her mom as his girl, even after nearly twenty years of marriage. *I love you* and *Take care of my girl* had been his last words to Amanda before she'd fled his room, unable to watch him die.

How badly had she let him down?

Shaking off the melancholy, Amanda watched as every gaze in the room shifted to Julia, some curious, some calculating. Did the information make them think better of Julia? Or worse of Rick?

Eternity broke the silence. "A good eye for beauty *and* sexiness. Tell us more, sugar. Is he as hot as he looks? Does he curl your toes? Make you lose consciousness?"

Julia's blush turned scarlet, but that didn't stop her eyes from widening. "Lose consciousness? Have you ever—"

Turning back to the mirror, Eternity picked up a pot of blush and a fat brush, studied her reflection, then set both down again. You couldn't improve on perfection, she often teased. "No," she said, then a slow, sexy smile curved her mouth, teeth gleaming white against glossy red lips. "But I've made it happen a time or two."

Tuning out the laughter, Amanda stepped behind the cheap silk screen that also served as a hanger and stripped out of her clothes. She wriggled into a red-and-white striped Brazilian thong, then added a breakaway skirt that looked like faded denim. The top was red, as well, two strips of fabric that cupped her breasts, then tied in the middle, leaving a few inches of dangling ruffles. The same small ruffles edged the material all the way around, including the off-the-shoulder cap sleeves. After letting her hair down, she left the privacy of the screen for a seat to put on six-inch heels with sexy ankle straps.

"Amanda's modest," Monique said to Julia with a sly wink. "I bet you are, too. I bet no one's seen you naked besides your mama, your boyfriends and your gynecologist."

"Nothing wrong with that," Eternity commented, and Amanda silently agreed. No one saw *her* naked, either, not since the last guy she'd dated, and that had been a very long time ago. So long that now she was coveting someone else's boyfriend.

Feeling as hot as Julia looked, Amanda stood. "I'm going to get some water. Anybody want any?"

A half dozen hands went up around the room. Ignoring the hint of panic in Julia's eyes, Amanda left the dressing room and headed for the bar. Rick wasn't working tonight, though he planned to be there when the club opened at seven. Otherwise, she would have asked one of the younger girls still wearing comfortable street shoes to get the water for her.

She hadn't gone farther than the end of the hall when her calf muscles started to protest. Maybe it had been the longer-than-usual run that morning, or the workouts she got with Julia, or maybe, she admitted with a smile, she was just getting old. Whatever the reason, she needed to do a few stretches before taking the stage to prevent a muscle spasm mid-dance. She'd seen it happen, and it wasn't a pretty sight.

"What are you grinning about?"

The smile faded when she saw Rick behind the bar. "I thought you were off tonight."

"I was, but Vincent called in sick."

Vincent, one of the other bartenders, often called in sick. The only reason Rosey didn't fire him was because they'd been together a long time. Sentimentality went a long way with their boss.

"Where's Julia?"

Amanda rested her hands on the polished wood bar. "Getting acquainted with the others. Eternity likes her."

"A lot of people like her. *I* like her."

Yeah. Me, too. "Can I have eight bottled waters?"

"Sure." But he didn't move to get them. He stayed where he was, leaning against the counter, arms folded over his chest. Unlike his girlfriend, he knew how to do casual. His jeans were faded practically white, his shirt was a rich russet shade and his belt was brown leather, well-worn. Between his amazing looks and body and his complete self-confidence, he could fit in anywhere in those clothes.

He freed one hand long enough to gesture in the general area of her breasts. "You doing a cowgirl thing tonight?"

She resisted the urge to adjust her top. As she'd told Julia, tugging at your clothes was a no-no. If you were going to wear revealing clothes, whether it was a stripper outfit on a club stage or a bikini on a public beach, then you should keep your hands away. Tugging just made you look self-conscious. The clothes covered what they covered, nothing more.

"Actually, I think of it as my Daisy Duke thing," she replied airily.

"That must go over well with your good-ole-Georgia-boy customers."

"They don't care much what I'm wearing. They're more interested in what I'm going to take off and when."

He shrugged as if that were a given. "What can I say? Men are scum."

"And you speak from experience."

"Yes, ma'am. I've been a man all my life. My old man was out of the picture long before he died, but my granddads and uncles stepped in to make sure my mother didn't have too calming an influence on my brothers and me. They succeeded."

"Your parents were divorced?" She aimed for an idle tone, but didn't know if she managed. Of course, she knew Sara and Gerald Calloway hadn't been divorced, but unless she was willing to let Rick know that she came from Copper Lake, she couldn't admit it.

And she didn't want Rick to know. Didn't want him to mention her to his mother, who might remember those poor Nelsons, or his brother, who would almost surely remember Randy Mandy. She'd hated that nickname, had hated Robbie and, for a time, had hated herself.

But the nickname and the memories were in the past, where they belonged. She wouldn't let them into the present.

"Nope, no divorce," Rick replied. "He just checked out. He was a lawyer and worked for the family businesses. He traveled a lot. Played a lot. He had better things to do than raise his kids. That was Mom's job."

"Did Mom know that before she had the three little devils?"

He grinned. "Aw, we weren't Satan. Just his spawn." Finally he pushed away from the counter, set a tray in front of her and began taking bottled water from the refrigerator two at a time. "Turned out there was a lot Mom didn't know until after the fact. That she was going to be a single mother long before he died. That he didn't have a clue what it meant to be faithful. That she'd wind up helping to raise his illegitimate son." His expression turned cynical. "At one point, he was married to my mom, engaged to Mitch's mother, who was pregnant with him at the time, and had a couple other women on the side."

"He was ambitious," Amanda commented quietly.

"He was scum." There was no teasing now. If Rick possessed any gentler feelings for his father, he was hiding them well.

She shifted the subject to something less resented. "So you get along with your father's illegitimate son?" She remembered Mitch Lassiter from his frequent visits to Copper Lake. In age, he came between Rick and Russ, and as far as looks, the family resemblance was there. Not as strong as between the three Calloway boys, but the connection between Mitch and the boys was apparent.

"Sure. Mitch is family."

She remembered that, too. Sara had acknowledged him as Gerald's son and, therefore, hers, and she'd corrected anyone who'd called him a stepson or half brother. Gerald had never been a father to Mitch, but Sara had certainly been a mother.

Rick twisted the cap off the last bottle of water and, instead of setting it on the tray, offered it to her. "What about you? Any brothers or sisters?"

"No, it's just me. My family's not nearly as interesting as yours. No infidelity, no trust issues, no lack of commitment."

"Just your quadriplegic father, your mother taking care of him, and you...taking care of her?"

After a sip of cold water, she shrugged. "I helped where I could." She'd handled the housework, the laundry, the cooking and the shopping. She'd read to her father, played his favorite music and sometimes even danced for him. He'd watched her with such emotion that too often she'd choked up. He had wanted so much for her—college, a career, a family and a home—and he'd believed she would get it all.

She'd graduated from college and her career was just weeks away. She had a home and a family was always possible. She'd fulfilled most of his dreams for her, but at what price? How disappointed would he have been by the choices she'd made to get from near-poverty in Copper Lake to where she was today?

This would break your daddy's heart, her mother had once told her. *I'm glad he's gone so he can't see what you've sunk to.*

The words had broken Amanda's heart.

"It must have been tough."

There was something in Rick's tone—sympathy, understanding, maybe even a bit of admiration—that made her stomach flip-flop and her fingers tremble. She curled them tightly to hold them steady and shrugged as if his tone didn't matter. "You do what you have to do."

That had been Brenda's mantra, but she'd been none too happy when Amanda had applied it to her dancing. There were other jobs, her mother had insisted, that didn't involve dancing half-naked for strangers and perverts.

There were. But Amanda *liked* dancing and it had helped her achieve a certain lifestyle.

Amanda glanced at the clock behind the bar. Ten minutes till seven. Chad would open the door soon, the early customers would wander in and the first dancers of the evening would take the three stages. "I'd better get back to the dressing room." Picking up the tray, setting a few bottles to wobbling, she murmured thanks and headed for the back.

She swore she could feel Rick's gaze on her until the stage door swung shut behind her. In the dressing room, she passed around the tray, setting the extra bottle in front of Julia, then sat down at her dressing table.

Thanks to the day's humidity, her curls were wilder than usual. She didn't try to tame them, but pulled them back on each side and secured them with a large silver comb.

Doing a cowgirl thing tonight? Rick had asked. Why not? She added silver earrings that dangled from her lobes, slid chunky silver rings on three fingers and a thumb, clipped conchas to the tie of her blouse and the tiny straps of her thong and circled her middle with a narrow chain linking tiny conchas.

"Did you like to play dress-up when you were little?"

She glanced at Julia as she slid a fringed suede band over her wrist to her upper arm. "I think I must have, because in the beginning, I got a real kick out of these clothes. Now, they're like your suits. Comfortable. Familiar."

"I can't imagine the day I'll be comfortable in a thong and a teeny bra," Julia said ruefully.

"It'll come. Trust me."

"'Trust me,'" Julia mimicked. "You sound like Rick."

Amanda met her gaze in the mirror. "Do you?"

"Trust Rick? With my life."

That was about as ringing as an endorsement could get. Amanda could see where he would inspire that kind of faith in Julia. She thought, with a few more personal conversations, he might inspire that kind of faith in her. He would be the first man since her father.

There was a rap at the open door, then Harry's gray head appeared around the corner. "It's seven o'clock. Eternity, Monique, Pilar, get out front." His gaze zeroed in on Julia. "You're not one of my girls."

Julia stiffened and flushed, looking as guilty as a ten-year-old caught ditching class. Amanda touched her shoulder reassuringly as she stood. "This is a friend of mine. Harry Clark, Julia Dautrieve. Harry manages this place and the dancers."

"And it's like trying to herd cats," he muttered. He looked Julia over head to toe, then grunted. With him, the grunt could mean anything from *Nice to meet you* to *Get the hell outta my club.* "Amanda, we've got a special this Saturday. You interested?"

She shook her head.

"Didn't think so." He looked at Julia again, gaze narrowed. With all five of Rosey's clubs under his control, Harry was always on the lookout for new prospects. Was he envisioning Julia as a prospect or hoping she wasn't? His next words answered that question. "I don't suppose your friend here—"

Amanda smiled politely. "No."

He grinned. "It never hurts to ask. You're on at seven-thirty." With that, he left the room again.

Julia was wide-eyed. "What was he talking about? What is a special?"

"Nothing you'd be interested in."

"Oh, Amanda, I'm interested in everything. Can't you tell by my wild and adventurous lifestyle?"

"Not this, you aren't." Amanda flipped open an eye kit and touched up the shadows that darkened her lids, then thickened and smudged her eyeliner. She added an extra coat of mascara to her upper lashes and a light dusting of apricot blush to her cheeks. After applying liner, lipstick and gloss to turn her mouth a shiny brownie-red pout, she looked up to find Julia watching her. Obviously still looking for pointers, it was clear Julia wasn't yet comfortable with her new makeup routine, but she would get there.

About the same time a thong became comfortable.

"Eternity and some of the others are going out after work. They invited us along. Want to go?"

Seven hours' work, then go out to party or home to

bed? There was no contest. "I don't think so. But you go ahead. You'll have a good time." Eternity was friendly and outgoing, but she wasn't a risk taker. The places she went were safe; the people she hung out with were law-abiding.

"You sure?"

"Yeah. I've got a date with my bed. But Eternity's fun. She'll entertain you *and* get you home safely before dawn."

Julia grinned, her eyes damn near sparkling. "Oh, wow. I'm going out with strippers. Isn't that cool?"

Chapter 5

He would fill in for Vincent, but not lock up. That was the deal Rick had made with Harry that got him out the door at 2:02. Harry was in the office, Chad was none-too-happily closing up and the women were all in the dressing room. Rick was betting Amanda would be the next one out the door and he was waiting for her.

He was lucky he was still able to stand after that first set she'd done. She'd taken inspiration from his comment and switched from Daisy Duke to cowgirl. She had strutted and sashayed all over the main stage, her movements so sexy and suggestive that she might as well have been wearing a sign that said, *Ride me, cowboy.*

There had been a fair number of men in the audience panting for a chance, along with one behind the bar.

She came out the exit, the light above gleaming on

her coppery hair, and took the steps two at a time. She was humming to herself, something classical. Stripper, lit teacher and Bach lover. Interesting package.

He let her unlock the car and toss her duffel in the backseat before he straightened in the shadows. "Hey, Amanda."

She might have tensed a bit. He couldn't be sure, because he was thinking every woman with a body like hers should be required to wear tight jeans cut low on the hips and skimpy shirts that left a lot of pale golden stomach bare. Why waste fabric covering something that really should be seen?

"Hey, Rick," she said at last. "Julia's in the dressing room."

"I know. She's going out with Eternity. I hear you turned them down."

"I'm too old to work and party in the same night."

He grinned. Old had never looked so good. "Julia said you said it was okay."

"Eternity's responsible. She'll keep an eye on her."

Did it occur to Amanda that they were talking about a thirty-three-year-old woman as if she were a child? Despite her naiveté and her stick-up-her-ass attitude, Julia had been in situations that would have scared Amanda spitless. But Julia did have that naiveté and the stick-up-her-ass attitude, and they somehow negated the tough, pistol-toting-cop side of her.

Amanda shifted, as if she wanted to get in her car and leave—*I've got a date with my bed,* she'd told Julia. He moved, too, taking a few steps toward her.

"You want to get some coffee?"

His question surprised her. She glanced at the club, nothing across the back but the door and cinder blocks painted tan. On the other side of those cinder blocks, though, was his live-in girlfriend, or so Amanda thought. Maybe he should have nixed the relationship idea from the start. It would have worked as well to say that Julia was just a friend—though that lacked a built-in deterrent to keep him and Amanda apart.

That would have been okay. He was deterrent enough.

"Aw, come on," he cajoled when she didn't answer. "They're going out partying. She'll be having fun. Besides, I bet you've never had coffee with the spawn of Satan."

Her smile was only about half-formed, a little mysterious, a whole lot interesting. "Don't count on it. Where?"

"There's an all-night pancake place a half mile west of here." It was the same place where he'd met Julia for their too-early meeting a few days earlier. Home of great pancakes, bad coffee and waitresses who had zero interest in their customers. Ideal.

"I'll meet you there."

As she got into her car and started the engine, he headed for the Camaro. He was halfway there when his cell rang. Fishing it from his pocket, he glanced at the caller ID, then flipped it open. "It's two-fifteen in the a.m. and I'm talking with a stripper. Why are you interrupting me?"

"What does she look like?" his youngest brother, Robbie, asked.

"She's the reason this place is called Almost Heaven."

"Just *almost?* Doesn't sound too hot."

Watching her dance was almost heaven. Dancing

with her—naked, in private, horizontal—that would be heaven. "What's up?"

"I'm on my way home from bailing Uncle Garry's secretary out of jail again and thought I'd give you a call, since you're the only person I know who's voluntarily awake at this ungodly hour on a weeknight. Hey, remember Kayla Conrad?"

Rick's pulse jumped, and he totally lost interest in why Uncle Garry's sixty-some-year-old grandmotherly secretary had been arrested. Kayla had lived across from the Calloway home when Rick was a teenager. Blond, beautiful, she had been the classic older woman for him. And Mitch. And Russ, plus at least half a dozen other guys in Copper Lake. They'd gone on to make plenty of other women happy, all thanks to Kayla.

"Yeah," he said, his tone almost reverent as he backed out of the parking space, then followed Amanda's car around the building. "I remember Kayla."

"She's getting married."

"Really? To someone we know?"

"Not well enough, Mom says. Tom Fitzgerald, the pastor at the church."

Kayla marrying a pastor. Rick never would have guessed that one. Of course, a week ago, he never would have guessed that he'd be wanting to hook up with a stripper.

"Anyway, some of us are taking him out for one last night on the town. We can't do it Friday night—he's got a wedding to perform—and, strange guy, he doesn't want to do it Saturday. Says he needs sleep before delivering the Sunday-morning sermon. So we're doing it a week from Friday. Want to join us?"

"If he's a good pastor, he had his 'one last night' a long time ago," Rick said before turning onto the street. "Sorry, man, I can't. I'm working." He didn't have a clue whether he was on the schedule for that night, but a lie was better than a night out with the good reverend, Robbie and his buddies.

"Yeah, yeah, you're always working. Who ever thought anyone would say that about you?"

Rick couldn't even take offense at the comment. He'd skated through school and had never held a job at a company that wasn't owned by his family until he'd graduated college. The family had always cut him a lot of slack and he'd taken advantage of it until he'd started his first job in law enforcement. He hadn't wanted any slack then. He'd loved it, from the first job with the Atlanta Police Department right up to the present.

"Well, I'm home now," Robbie said. "Maybe I'll see you next weekend."

"Yeah, give me a call."

"And call Mom. She misses your ugly mug."

"I will. Later, Rob." Slowing, Rick eased into a parking space that fronted the restaurant's plate-glass windows and flipped his phone off. Amanda's car was parked two spaces down, and she waited for him on the sidewalk, a jacket folded over her arm.

Damn, she was pretty. Just as Kayla Conrad had been every boy's teenage fantasy, Amanda had to be every conscious man's fantasy. The way she looked, the way she moved, the way she smiled…everything about her was so damn *good*.

He was undercover, he reminded himself as he got out of the car. She could be dirty. He was supposed to be committed to Julia.

When he stepped onto the curb, he caught a whiff of her perfume—sweet, spicy, exotic. It held its own against the smells of heavy foods from the restaurant and traffic on the street. Her hair was held by a band at the crown of her head, and the heels that made her legs look incredible had been traded for sandals with narrow straps and thin soles.

Hell, her legs were incredible with or without heels. Even in jeans.

"Ride 'em, cowgirl," he said in greeting as she fell into step with him.

"And here I thought you'd be thinking I was thinking, 'Ride me, cowboy.'"

"Yeah, the words did cross my mind at one point. Must have been the naughty things you were doing with that pole. About the time the guy shouted out that *he* had something long and hard for you."

"Like I haven't heard that one before," she murmured as she walked through the door he was holding for her. The air inside was ten degrees cooler than outside. She shrugged into her jacket as the hostess came to seat them.

Their booth was brightly lit, in the middle of the dining room. The closest other diners were a family, parents and three kids, looking worn-out, dazed, probably traveling somewhere on the cheap.

"Unless you're a fan of really bad coffee, I'd get something else to drink."

"So you come here often."

"I bring all my dates here."

The reminder of his number-one date—his one and only, if it had been the real thing—made her blink. Julia's claim on him meant something to her. She didn't poach. Even this—an innocent meeting, nothing but coffee, with Julia knowing about the whole thing—made her uncomfortable.

Was it because her parents had had a long, happy marriage? Ironic, when his own commitment to fidelity had come from his parents' long *un*happy marriage.

The waitress took their orders—Coke for him, along with a fat, gooey cinnamon roll; Diet Coke for her—then left them alone. After a moment's silence, Amanda said, "Julia seemed to have a good time tonight."

"Are you kidding? She was like a kid in a candy store. She's always been the good girl. She never argued, never talked back, never got her clothes dirty, never skipped school, never exceeded the speed limit, never, never, never. Now she's getting a chance to hang out with the…"

"Bad girls," Amanda supplied.

"Well…yeah. And it turns her on." Damn. Bad choice of words. Last thing he needed was to think about turn-ons with the biggest, hottest turn-on of all sitting across from him.

Face warm—though not necessarily from embarrassment—he shrugged. "What I'm trying to say is—"

"You said it fine. This is her chance to step outside

her comfort zone, to do things she's never done before, to become a person she's never been before. Everyone should try it at least once."

Tension draining from his neck muscles, he asked, "What's outside your comfort zone?"

She smiled at the waitress as she delivered their drinks and his roll, then meticulously removed her straw from its paper, tearing one tip, sliding it loose, creasing it flat before folding it in quarters. "I don't think anything's outside my comfort zone. I'm a stripper, remember? A bad girl. One step above scum of the earth."

Rick paused in the act of slicing a chunk of icing-drizzled roll with his fork. "Did your mother tell you that?"

"Her sister."

"And what qualifies her to make that judgment? Is she a psychologist? Psychiatrist? Sociologist? Arbiter of all that's good and evil in the world?"

"She'd like to think so."

He scooped up the first bite of roll and offered it to her, but she shook her head. "So what's outside your comfort zone? Besides meeting my mother," he said before filling his mouth.

"Not just your mother. Any mothers. They tend to look at me and see a bad influence." She sipped her diet pop, gazing into the distance, then refocused. "Going to college was. Teaching will be. Going back to the dreary little nameless town where I grew up would be *way* outside my comfort zone."

"Hey, I'm from that same town. Mine's an hour east of here. Where is yours?"

"Between the middle of nowhere and the end of the line."

The roll was so good that it made up for the bad coffee he'd had last time. Rick ate a third of it before speaking again. "You'll do fine teaching. The girls will all want to be like you, and the boys will all want to be with you."

"I was thinking if I cut my hair, got glasses and borrowed some of Julia's suits…"

"The boys would still notice. It's a hormonal thing." He ate the last bite he could hold of the roll, then sat back and studied her. He would hate to see her cut her hair, though he didn't know how she stood it in Atlanta's hot, humid summers. The weight and stickiness must be unbearable…but it was damned sexy.

She shifted under his gaze. Took a long drink of pop. Folded her hands together on the tabletop. Moved them to her lap. Finally, when she was starting to really get on edge, he broke the quiet and changed the subject. "Julia mentioned a special this Saturday. What is that?"

She blinked a couple of times, then apparently recalled the brief conversation with Harry in the dressing room. "Haven't you ever worked any?"

He shook his head.

"They're just private events. Bachelor parties, birthday parties, private dances for small groups. Things like that. Harry provides the girls and the bartender and pretty much anything goes."

Anything, Rick knew, meant just that. Prostitution, sex games, threesomes, gangbangs. *Didn't think you'd be interested,* Harry had told Amanda. Good.

"How's the money?" he asked casually.

"Better than a night at the club. The customers are usually celebrating a special occasion, so they're willing to splurge. Some of the dancers like them. Some don't."

"What about Tasha? Did she do them?" The instant the name left his mouth, Rick knew he'd made a mistake. There was nothing obvious in Amanda's reaction—the tightening of her jaw was subtle, the narrowing of her gaze minimal—but she was instantly suspicious.

She drained the last of the pop from her glass, leaned back against the cushions and settled her attention on him. Her voice was quieter when she spoke, stiffer. "Exactly what is your interest in Tasha?"

He clasped his hands together on top of the table. "I don't know. I don't even know her. We talked for maybe a couple minutes. But there was just something so young about her. Vulnerable. She reminded me…"

He didn't flinch under her gaze but held it as if there was nothing more—or less—to the answer he'd given. Let her think there had been someone vulnerable and young in his past. Let her think he had a soft streak toward some of the girls, as she did.

"She's nineteen," Amanda said at last.

"Which can be a lot younger for some kids than for others."

She acknowledged her own words with a nod. "Tasha was pretty tough for her age. She'd wanted to be an exotic dancer since she was thirteen. Once she made it, she loved it. She was proud of her job, her success. If someone gave her a hard time, she gave it right back."

"Sometimes tough is just an act."

"And sometimes it's the real thing." Then she grinned.

"Of course, men thinking a girl is vulnerable is usually a good thing in this business. You get a half dozen guys who want to take care of you, and you've got some damn good tips."

Rick scowled. "I can tell the difference between an act and the real thing."

Her grin matched his scowl in intensity. "That's what most men think. A flutter of the lashes, a breathy little voice, a little helplessness in the manner and men think, 'I can rescue her. I can be her hero and take care of her.' And all it costs is whatever he has to spend."

"I'm not interested in being anyone's hero."

"Too bad. You could probably do it well."

He tried to swallow, but his throat was dry. A gulp of watered-down pop didn't help much. His voice was still raspy. "Okay, so a woman who likes to manipulate gullible guys won't have any trouble finding plenty to use. I'm not gullible. There was just something about Tasha…"

"That got under your skin. It happens sometimes." She breathed deeply and her brow wrinkled as if she were trying hard to think. "Yeah, Tasha did the specials. Her and DinaBeth and maybe four or five others from the other clubs. Tasha looked on them as less time on her feet, more money at the end of the night. In her life, everything was for sale—her dances, her companionship, her body."

"Hard to believe she'd just walk away from such a good market for what she was selling."

"Like she said, she got a better offer." Amanda paused, then corrected herself. "Like Harry said. No one talked to her besides him."

Harry had said the same about DinaBeth a few weeks earlier and about Lisa a month before that. "Don't you think it's odd that someone who loved her job, who was proud of it, just walked away from it without a word to anyone?"

Amanda tapped her nails on the table. "A lot of the friendships you make in this business aren't long-term. Over the years, I've danced with at least a hundred different girls, but I was really friends with maybe three or four. I remember faces, some names, but I don't stay in touch. I don't celebrate holidays with them. I don't know where they are or what they're doing. And I doubt they ever think of me and say, 'I wonder whatever happened to Amanda.'"

"But you said DinaBeth and Tasha were friends. Did Tasha keep in touch with DinaBeth after *she* left?"

Tiring of the slow, rhythmic tap, Amanda stilled her fingers and called an image of Tasha to mind. As usual, DinaBeth was nearby. They danced together, partied together and had even, on one occasion, vacationed together. They'd gone to New Orleans for Mardi Gras and brought back enough tacky beads to go around.

Yeah, they'd been friends. But Tasha had been surprised by DinaBeth's leaving. *She would have told me,* she'd protested to Harry when he'd told them DinaBeth had quit. *She told me everything.*

Amanda had seen so many girls come and go that she'd long ago stopped being surprised. She'd worked more than a few clubs herself where she'd given notice as she walked out the door. She was an independent contractor. Notice was a courtesy, not a requirement.

But she'd never left any friends behind without saying goodbye.

"I don't know if they stayed in touch. I'd guess no." She hesitated, nerves tightening, then asked, "Do you think something happened to Tasha?"

Rick's features were set in an even, give-nothing-away mask. "A nineteen-year-old girl who loves her job walks away one night and never comes back? What do you think?"

Security was always a problem for strippers—less so at Rosey's clubs than elsewhere, but still a problem. A lot of girls used stage names and didn't give their personal information to anyone, not even the other dancers. Sometimes overeager customers decided to wait outside the club to have a one-on-one with a dancer in private. Some customers tried to buy addresses or even went so far as to follow a dancer home.

But neither Tasha nor DinaBeth had ever complained about trouble with a customer. Friendly or not, that was information they would have shared with the other girls.

They had merely done what countless dancers before them had—changed their minds and moved on without wasting time on goodbyes. The only difference was Rick, asking questions when no one else had been the least bit curious.

Had he been truthful when he'd said there was just something about Tasha? Had there really been someone similar in his own life, someone she reminded him of? Despite his denials, had he thought he could be the one to rescue her?

Or had he had something going on with her? A

dancer and a bartender hooking up wasn't uncommon. Granted, he was practically old enough to be Tasha's father, but that wasn't at all uncommon, either. He might even have admitted it if Amanda hadn't put him on the defensive first by pointing out her age.

A shiver rocketed through her, and she pulled her jacket tighter. "I should probably go."

He stretched out one hand but didn't try to make contact with her. "We can change the subject if it's making you uncomfortable."

"It's not the subject. It's you. Hundreds of dancers have walked away without goodbyes and never included those of us left behind in their new lives. The only difference this time is that here you are, asking a lot of questions about a girl you say you hardly knew. If you hardly knew her, what the hell difference does it make?"

For a long time they stared, his gaze as steady as hers wasn't. Finally he broke it to look at the check and slide to his feet. Then he pulled a ten from his wallet, laid it next to the check and gestured for her to rise. She did and headed for the door, for warmer temperatures and cleaner air and the security of her car only a few feet away.

As soon as they stepped outside, he spoke. "There was a girl—pretty, smart, brash. Her family didn't have much money and when her father died, they pretty much split up. She came here, looking for a job that would make life just a little bit easier, and wound up onstage in a club. Just for one week, she said, but the money was better than she'd ever seen. She'd stay two weeks, save all her tips and then quit. Then it became a month, two months, until one day she just disappeared. No one ever knew what happened to her.

"Today she's been pretty much forgotten, by the people who knew her as a pretty, smart girl, by the family who didn't approve of what she was doing, by the dancers she worked with night after night at the club. Call me sentimental, but I think a person should be remembered by *someone*. She shouldn't have to pass through life and be forgotten as if she never existed."

"You remember," Amanda said quietly. Had he dated the girl? Befriended her? No, wait, it was Copper Lake. He might have lied to, used and betrayed someone from the wrong side of town, but he wouldn't have been friends with her.

"I don't understand how a nineteen-year-old girl can disappear and no one thinks anything of it."

"Haven't you ever wanted to change your life? To wake up living someplace else, doing something else, being someone else?"

"No...but there've been a few times I wouldn't mind sending my brother off someplace else." He slanted her a look. "Have you?"

"Of course." Then, before she could stop it, the question was out. "Which brother?"

"Robbie. The youngest. You can't imagine what a pain in the ass he was as a kid."

Oh, he was wrong there. She didn't have to imagine. She knew.

Rather than remember her experience with the youngest Calloway, she returned to his question. "Of course I want to change my life. But I chose to do it the old-fashioned way—going to school, getting a job, making myself over into a respectable member of the community. It's taken the better part of twelve years. Some people want quicker results. DinaBeth was sure that if she made it to Hollywood, some blockbuster producer was going to take one look and splash her face across a forty-foot screen. She never did any school plays or community theater. She never took any acting or voice lessons. She wanted to be an overnight success. That's probably where she is—Hollywood—and she probably conned Tasha into joining her there."

Of that whole speech, he fixed on one brief comment. "You don't need that degree or that job to make you respectable. You're the most respectable woman I know next to my mother."

It wasn't the damn near schmaltzy words that got to her, or even the mention of Sara, who was considered a saint by both the community and her sons for having raised them. God knows, the closest to *saint* Amanda had gotten was its opposite. *Taking your clothes off for strange men makes you the worst of sinners, Amanda. My daughter, the stripper, the sinner, the tempter of vile men.*

And my mother, Amanda thought, melodramatic and over-the-top.

Her sins aside, what got to her about Rick's statement was the sincerity in his voice, in his eyes. She knew it could be faked, just as she knew this wasn't. He believed what he said and so did she; it sent a shaky feeling through her. What did you do when a man paid you the greatest compliment you'd ever gotten? When he was living with a woman you admired and liked? When even talking with him made you feel as if you were betraying that woman?

"Thank you, Rick," she said softly. With that and a polite nod, she went to her car, undoing the lock as she approached.

He waited until she was about to slide behind the wheel to say, "I'll follow you home."

"You don't have to," she said automatically, but he waved her off and got into his own car. It was two forty-five in the morning, and he wanted to make sure she got home all right.

Oh, yeah, he could be a great hero. If he ever got interested.

Despite the light traffic, she drove the speed limit, ever conscious of his headlights three car lengths behind her. When she turned into her driveway, he pulled to the curb, shut off the engine and got out.

"You don't have to see me to the door." How long had it been since *that* had happened? A lifetime. She'd been young, as naive as Julia. But she'd grown up quickly.

"My brothers and I may be the spawn of Satan, but we're gentlemanly spawn."

She climbed the steps, unlocked and opened the door. Dancer was waiting on the other side, eager for a trip outside. Halfway down the steps, the dog paused, eyes even with Rick's, and gave him a look, then continued into the yard.

"At least she didn't pee on me," he joked.

"Yeah, that's always a good thing." Amanda set her bag and purse on the floor inside the door, then turned back.

He still stood on the middle step, hands in his hip

pockets, looking at her as if…she didn't know. Didn't want to know. Damn sure didn't want to know if she was looking back at him the same way.

The porch lights cast yellow-tinged light over the wicker, the painted floorboards and him while leaving her in shadow. He had some years on his face—no one would mistake him for being on the young side of thirty—but they'd been good years. He looked as if he'd never had a real care in the world.

Had never been poor. Had never been disowned by his family. Had never been called names too vile for any parent to use with their child. Had never worried about living alone and lonely.

Though he'd lived with Gerald the philanderer. He'd been as disappointed in his father as she'd been in her mother. As her mother had been in her. He'd surely had his upsets, his failures. He didn't look it, though.

She wanted to be as carefree.

"Well…" Rick's voice was gravelly and low.

If this had been a date, he would have come onto the porch, would have tried to kiss his way inside the house and into her bed.

If this had been a date, she would have let him.

But it wasn't a date and she was glad he kept his distance or she might be tempted to forget it. Might forget Julia, too. Might try to tempt him.

"Thanks for the Coke," she said as Dancer trotted up the steps again, passing Rick without a glance.

"Thanks for the company." He backed down the steps and lifted one hand in a wave before spinning. "See you later."

She went inside, latching the screen door as he got in his car, locking the door as he drove away. The house felt empty with no one but Dancer to break the stillness. "Not that you aren't the best company in the world," she said aloud, giving the dog a scratch behind the ear. It was just that she felt…well, empty. She wanted friends. A boyfriend. Someday a husband and maybe even kids. None of those things had been priorities, she'd told Rick, and that was true. For twelve years, all she'd focused on was saving money, getting her degree and finding a job. Well, she had a nice chunk of change in mutual funds, plus a little play money in high-risk, high-yield bonds. She had the degree and the job was hers, starting after Christmas.

Now she wanted a man. Someone else's man.

And unless she'd misjudged that *look* a few moments ago, there might be a chance she could have him.

Saturday nights were big nights at Always Heaven. Every girl who showed up for the evening got her turn onstage, then mingled with the customers. That, Rick knew, was where they made their real money. Tips tucked into bras or thongs onstage were nice, but it was sitting at the tables and giving lap and private dances in the back room that paid the bills.

And since Saturday nights were good for the dancers, they were good for the bartenders, as well. Not that Rick got to keep any of it. His salary and tips went from his pocket to GBI, and the tips were often more than the salary.

He was working the bar with Vincent tonight. On weeknights, one bartender was enough. The customers drank a lot of booze, but their primary interest was the girls. On weekends, it took two to keep the booze flowing.

Vincent was in his mid-forties, thin in a bony scarecrow way, with sunken eyes and a head of hair styled to do Johnny Cash proud. He was on the lazy side, and he had an in of some kind with Rosey Hines. He also had a thing—unrequited, Rick was sure—for Eternity.

During a lull when Amanda, Eternity and an Asian girl named Anh took the stages, Rick shifted the toothpick he chewed on to one side of his mouth and went to stand next to Vincent. "I heard Mr. Hines has a special scheduled for tonight. Does he do that very often?"

His narrow gaze riveted on Eternity, Vincent shrugged. "From time to time."

"I want to get in on it."

"Why?"

"Same reason the girls do." Rick nodded toward the stage but was careful to keep from actually seeing Amanda. She remained a blur of pale golden skin, blue garments and sensuous moves. "Money."

"Where'd you hear about it?"

"Being a good listener is one of the job requirements for tending bar."

Anyone else might have cracked a smile, smirked or had some kind of comeback. Vincent gave no sign he'd even heard. "Mr. Hines chooses the personnel for the specials. If he wants you there, he'll let you know."

"Why aren't you there tonight? He didn't want you?"

Finally Vincent looked at Rick, his blue gaze colder, narrower than usual. Eternity probably felt a moment's ease as the creep factor for her ratcheted down. Rick's own creep factor just about doubled, making him grateful for the pistol strapped to his ankle. "I've done plenty of specials. I'll do plenty more in the future. Tonight I decided to be here."

Because Eternity was here? Before Rick could do more than wonder, Vincent walked to the far end of the bar and turned his back to him.

Rick filled a couple of drink orders, wiped the bar a time or two, watched the second hand on the clock make a few rotations, then finally looked at Amanda. Because there was nothing left to do. Because it was totally natural to look at a half-naked woman on display. Because he couldn't have *not* looked at her for one minute longer.

She wore a halter top, royal blue and clinging as if it were two sizes too small, with a skirt, also blue, made of some gauzy fabric. The hem was uneven, dipping lower in the center and rising high on the outside, and it fluttered around her runner's thighs with every move she made.

This was the first song in her three-song set. Before it was over, she would remove the top. By the end of the second song, she would remove the skirt, and she would finish the set wearing nothing but bits of fabric covering the most intimate parts of a body meant to drive him nuts.

God, he needed a drink.

When she pulled off the top to reveal a bra that was tiny enough and flimsy enough to make a joke of the name, he bit the toothpick in half. When she removed the skirt, one agonizing inch at a time, and he saw the matching panty that was a shade smaller than decent, with ties that crisscrossed her hips before tying in a delicate bow right across her belly button, he damn near bit his tongue in half.

Aw, man, this was *not* the way he worked. Not once in fourteen years in law enforcement had he ever gotten turned on in the course of his job. Not once had he forgotten for even one second what he was there for, that he was the good guy and everybody else, whether bad guy or innocent bystander, was off-limits. He was undercover, for God's sake.

And he wanted to get wild and dirty under the covers with Amanda.

One good reminder that he needed to get his head straight chose that moment to come to the bar. Julia had been seated at a table in the corner, watching everything, her encyclopedic brain taking it all in and cataloging it.

Amanda had already changed Julia's hairstyle and makeup. Rick assumed he was seeing her influence in Julia's clothes tonight, as well. She wore jeans, but they were a world apart from the previous night's pair. These were faded, tight enough to make loss of consciousness a real possibility and long enough to require four-inch heels. *I'm getting used to them,* Julia had told him when he'd first commented on them. *For the night I audition.*

Ms. Stick-up-her-ass had certainly changed her attitude in the past few days.

She'd come home at five in the morning, fumbling loudly enough at the door to wake him. He'd grabbed his pistol and taken up a defensive posture at the end of the hallway, only to relax when she'd come through the door. *Oh,* she'd said. *What are you doing up?*

She'd swayed a bit as she'd closed the door and secured

the three locks. *The girls think I'm tipsy, but I'm not.* And as easily as turning off a switch, she'd straightened and, utterly steady on her feet, strolled past him to her room.

Damn, Julia had *never* strolled.

She leaned her elbows on the bar, showing a nice bit of skin in the vee of her snug shirt. "Give me a twenty-dollar glass of wine."

"Yeah, right." He pulled a bottled water from the refrigerator and slid it across to her. "Our cheapest wine is twenty-*five* dollars a glass. You learning anything?"

"Uh-huh." She didn't offer anything more, but turned to watch the room. "I'm starting to think that actually dancing won't be nearly as intimidating as chatting up the customers."

"You talk to people all the time."

"I interview." Her voice lowered. "I interrogate. I don't chat."

"It's not like you're expected to carry on intelligent conversation. You flutter your lashes, use a breathy little voice, act helpless and you've got it made."

Julia quirked one brow. "And you learned that... Ah, having coffee with Amanda. What other secrets did she tell you?"

He moved to the center of the bar to fill an order, then returned, leaning across the bar. To anyone who saw them, they'd look intimate, but all he really wanted was privacy. "Both Tasha and DinaBeth liked doing the specials. We need to find out if Lisa did, too. Maybe the connection is more than just the club. Maybe it's got something to do with those."

"I'll have someone get in touch with Lisa's sister."

"When do you audition?"

Finally, a glimpse of the Julia he knew. She swallowed hard and something flashed through her dark eyes. "Tomorrow night. Since it's illegal to sell liquor on Sundays, the club's not busy and Harry will have time." She looked away, then back. "You'll be off."

Illegal to sell liquor, Rick thought, but they did it anyway, at least to their regulars.

Auditions weren't formal. A girl came in, talked to Harry, he put her on one of the smaller stages, she danced and if he liked her or thought his customers would he gave her a shot. She could pay her seventy-five-buck house fee like all the rest and hope to make more.

"You don't want me here?" he asked with a grin.

"No."

"Aw, come on…"

She shot him a sharp look.

Truth was, he'd rather not sit in on her audition. He had to work with her when this case was over. He'd rather not know what she looked like in stripper clothes. He'd really rather not find out just how much she'd learned.

"You comfortable being in here alone?"

Another sharp look. "I can take care of myself."

He leaned close enough to smell her perfume. The other prim stuff in her life might be temporarily banished, but the perfume was as sweet and innocent as cotton candy. "I don't think you can hide a pistol or pepper spray in those outfits you bought."

"Amanda will be here, and Eternity. They're enough."

"What will Amanda think when you have your big debut and I'm not here to see it?"

"She'll think what we tell her to think."

Rick reached for another toothpick. Chewing on them was a habit that had driven his mother crazy. *When are you going to stop that?* she'd once asked, and he'd quickly replied, *The day I take up smoking.* She'd never said anything about it since.

"People don't tell Amanda what to think," he pointed out. Though he might like to see someone try.

Julia fluttered a hand. "She'll think I want to give you a private show."

At home. In his bedroom. Ending in wild, wicked, incredibly hot sex.

He wasn't a horny kid anymore. He knew wild, wicked, incredibly hot sex happened, but not every time. Not with every woman. Most of the time sex was good. It was great. But it didn't usually turn him inside out. And truthfully, sex with Julia sounded about as much a turn-on as kissing the sister he didn't have.

But sex with Amanda… He watched her disappear from the stage, knowing she would come out again in a moment or two and circle through the audience. Someone would ask her to sit with him a while and buy her a drink. She would order her usual—water—and he'd get charged the eighteen-dollar minimum for it. She would listen more than she would talk and she would smile a lot and he would think that maybe, just maybe, he could be the one to make a difference in her life. For a few minutes, he could live the fantasy that he could have her. She could be his. He could be the one to rescue her.

Rick knew she didn't need rescuing. But he wouldn't mind at all being her hero.

"About that..." Julia took a drink, then tightly screwed the lid back on the bottle. "I'm thinking that after I get the job, we should break up."

She couldn't have said much that would have surprised him more. "Break up?"

"You're getting cozy with Amanda. I'm getting cozy with Eternity and Monique. We don't need to be together anymore."

Nah. Uh-uh. She was one of the things keeping him from making that fantasy reality. He didn't want to break up. Didn't want to be available in any way, shape or form.

"It's really pretty limiting," Julia went on, not seeming to notice that he was staring at her. "I needed an in and I've got it. Now I need to be free to take full advantage of it."

"I'm holding you back from that?"

"Having a boyfriend who works here is. Besides, they've noticed that you and Amanda..." She finished with a shrug.

"That we what?"

"That you take breaks when she does. That sometimes you're waiting out back when she leaves. That you two went out for coffee after work Thursday night. They don't think Amanda would do anything wrong. They just think—" she smiled unexpectedly "—you would."

"You went out drinking," he protested.

"I know, but I was with the girls. You were with one girl. And it wasn't your live-in girlfriend."

"Because you went out drinking with the other girls."

She smiled in that smug, condescending way women had with men when there was no logic to their arguments but it didn't matter because they were going to win anyway. "It won't even be a big breakup. We've been together a long time, we've been growing apart, we thought moving in together might bring us closer, but now we've come to the conclusion that we want out of the relationship. No one's hurt, no one's holding a grudge, we're still friends."

No logic. If Rick had really been seeing a woman for three years and was living with her, it was a sure bet that a breakup, even a mutually-agreed-upon one, would leave some hard feelings.

She patted his hand. "We weren't really fooling anyone. They must think we're the most unaffectionate couple in the entire world. We just don't act the way lovers should. There's no chemistry."

He gave her a narrow scowl and muttered, "Go ahead. Trample my ego."

"If anyone's ego can survive trampling, it's yours."

Her logic might be skewed—more like nonexistent—but he couldn't find fault with her conclusion. She needed to be chummy with as many of the dancers as possible and, since none of them were involved seriously with just one man, a boyfriend could be a hassle. And there *was* no chemistry between them. Hadn't he just thought that sex with Julia would be worth skipping out on?

Truth was, breaking up was good for the case. He would lose her as his buffer, but what she might learn by insinuating herself more closely with the dancers was more important than helping him resist his personal temptations.

"Okay," he agreed. "But you'll stay at the apartment."

"*Yee*-ah," she said in a nice imitation of the younger dancers' sarcasm. "I don't want anyone here knowing where I really live. I'll tell Amanda tonight. And I'm going out with Eternity and Monique again tonight. Okay?"

When he nodded, she squeezed his hand, then returned to her table, greeting several girls on the way. She was going to fit in here better than anyone had imagined.

And him? His life was about to get a whole lot harder.

Chapter 6

When break time came, Amanda headed for her tiny closet at the back of the building. Her reading glasses and book were already on the table. She set down two miniature candy bars and a bottle of water, removed her eight-inch heels and sat on the chaise with a sigh.

It had been a good night. It was only a little more than half over and she'd already pocketed more than eight hundred dollars in tips. But for a nickel, she'd go home right then and spend the next two hours in a hot bath. Then she smiled wryly. Sure, she would. This job was all about the money and saving enough of it to have the life she'd always wanted. There was no such thing as too much money.

She looked at the glasses and the book, then reached for one of the candy bars. Chocolate was surely the next best thing in the world to dancing. And sex. And personal satisfaction. It was a shame that, in quantity, it went straight to her hips, a bigger shame that the time when hips were a good thing was long past.

After peeling open the wrapper, she took one sweet, luscious bite and the door opened, catching her in the act. Expecting Rick, she was tempted to swallow without savoring, but she resisted. Good thing, since it wasn't Rick.

Julia stood in the doorway, her pose amazingly casual for the uptight woman she'd been just a few days earlier. "Can I come in?"

"Sure." Amanda wasn't in the mood to read anyway. Chewing the candy slowly, she swung her feet to the floor and made room for Julia to join her on the chaise.

Instead of lounging back as Amanda did, Julia sat on the edge of the cushion, feet together, spine straight. Amanda had never seen her slump or slouch. That must have been some ballet teacher, for her lessons to have stuck so long.

"Rick and I broke up."

The announcement came as Amanda was swallowing and she choked, coughing hard before gulping down a mouthful of water.

Julia absently patted her on the back. "It's been coming for a while. We've been together a long time and we've gotten pretty platonic. We thought moving in together might fix whatever was wrong, but I've had my own room the whole time. We're just not relating."

After another sip of water, Amanda said, "I'm sorry."

She was, even though a small devil was doing cart-wheels in her stomach.

"Oh, don't be. I'm not." Finally Julia slid back, relaxing against the wall. "I'm relieved. I like Rick a lot and I'd rather end it now when we can still be friends. The last guy I broke up with—I used his photograph for target practice at the gun range. I would have shot him for real if I'd thought I could get away with it. He was scum."

After a moment, Amanda said, "You don't seem at all upset about this breakup."

"No, really, I'm not. We've been living pretty much as roommates for a while. In fact, now we really will be roommates. I plan to stay at the apartment until I find a new place to live."

Amanda thought back to her few serious relationships. While she'd never wanted to drill her exes' pictures with bullet holes, they hadn't been friends before they started dating and there had certainly been no reason to become friends after they'd stopped. She couldn't imagine continuing to live together. She would rather sleep in her car.

Though, since she would never give up her house for any man, she wouldn't have to worry about that. She would just kick his ass out.

"Hey, we're going out tonight to celebrate my freedom," Julia said. "Want to go?"

"You and Rick?"

"No." *Of course not,* her tone said. "Eternity, Monique, Rica and that cute little girl who makes me look like a bean pole."

"Halle," Amanda supplied. She was twenty-four,

although she looked younger, and only a few inches over five feet, but with curves that could make any man dizzy.

"Yeah, Halle. Want to join us?"

"No, thanks. I took myself off the party circuit a long time ago," Amanda said, but her thoughts were elsewhere. What about Rick? How would he celebrate his freedom? Hitting the clubs, drinking, maybe picking up a pretty stranger? He'd been saying no to all the dancers ever since he'd come to work at Almost Heaven. Would he surprise one of them by finally saying yes?

Would he say yes to Amanda?

No, because she wasn't asking. She wasn't interested in a long-term relationship and she'd taken herself off the casual-flings circuit a long time ago. Even if she wanted either, she had no desire to be any man's rebound lover.

"I'd better get back to work," she said, strapping on her shoes again. "You guys have fun—and don't overdo it. Your audition's tomorrow."

Julia flushed, but managed a smile, too. "I'm almost starting to look forward to it."

"You'll do fine." Amanda's friend had told her that at her own audition twelve years ago and it had gone without a hitch. She'd been scared, but overall it had been painless. "You were great at the house yesterday afternoon."

"From your lips to Harry's ears." Julia raised both hands, fingers crossed, then led the way from the room. As Amanda switched off the light and closed the door, Julia said, "I really think you should consider doing something with Rick tonight. Have a late dinner or an early breakfast…or a *late* breakfast."

Amanda laughed. "You're trying to set your ex up with someone else on the same night you became exes?"

"Not someone else. You. You're special."

Unexpectedly Amanda's eyes grew damp. The only person besides her father who had ever told her that was Robbie Calloway, and he'd been lying. The whole time he was being so sweet to her, spending time with her, he'd been telling lies about her. He was the one who'd started calling her Randy Mandy. He was the one who'd made her school life miserable.

But Rick wasn't like his brother. She'd learned a lot about men since Robbie and she knew Rick was a good one. No doubt, he'd broken plenty of hearts, but he didn't do it with deceit and cruelty. He didn't do it for fun. Julia said she would trust him with her life.

Easier to trust someone with your life than with your heart.

"Thanks. It's nice to be popular." Though she smiled, long-ago bitterness stirred inside her. The cool kids in school hadn't known her name until Robbie made a fool of her, but she was popular here. Men liked her so damn much they visited regularly to ogle her body and to buy a little of her time.

And though she was anything but cheap, at that very moment, she felt it.

She and Julia separated once they returned to the bar. She made eye contact with each man she passed, smiling at them, getting smiles and assessing looks in return. A man sitting alone at a table in the middle of the room gave her the smile, the look, then laid a fifty-dollar bill on the table.

She sat down, scooping up the money and tucking it away in one long, smooth move. "Hi, I'm Amanda."

His name was Bradley, and he was in town for a convention. He was good-looking, probably around fifty, and wore an expensive suit, expensive cologne and a wedding ring on his left hand. He was like a thousand other customers before him: he liked to talk about himself, he was generous with his money and probably little, if any, of what he said was true.

But she listened, smiling, nodding, making him feel as if he were the only thing of interest in her life at that moment. And he was. He'd bought her time, which meant he'd also bought her attention. But that didn't keep her from noticing Rick behind the bar or from feeling his gaze slide over her again and again.

You really should consider doing something with Rick tonight. Did he know Julia was trying to find him a date? Probably not. He didn't need any help in that arena. He was gorgeous, sexy, had a killer body and, for people who cared about those sorts of things, came from a proud and very successful Georgia family. He was small-town royalty.

She didn't care about those sorts of things.

She finished her time with Bradley, danced another set, then spent an hour with a grandfatherly type who was lonely rather than a lech. He came to the club twice a month, dropped a bundle on Amanda and Eternity and left smiling. Who said money couldn't buy happiness?

On Friday and Saturday nights, the club stayed open until three. Amanda was grateful when closing time arrived. Pretty much everything on her hurt, she reflected as she changed into street clothes and blessed flats. Julia again extended the invitation to celebrate with her, and Amanda again turned her down. She couldn't have partied tonight for love or money—and she was a person who knew the value of both.

"Have fun and be careful," she said as she slung her duffel strap over her shoulder.

"Eternity will see that she gets home safe and sound," Eternity said with a lecherous smile and a wink.

Amanda said goodbye and left the building, breathing the cool, humid air deeply. She loved Atlanta. Loved the crowdedness, the endless choices of things to do. Loved the Old South graciousness and the opportunities and the beauty. Loved that it wasn't Copper Lake. If she'd had to stay in her hometown, she wouldn't have survived. Couldn't have.

She smelled Rick before she saw him, saw him before she heard him. He was leaning against his car, parked next to hers. The street lamp above buzzed and drew a cloud of insects, turning him into an intriguing form of light and shadow, showing his somber expression.

She watched him a moment, barely able to hear his slow, steady breathing, but she didn't speak and neither did he. After a time, she got into her car, well aware that he was moving to get into his. She started the engine and felt the powerful rumble of his as it roared to life. She drove out of the parking lot, knowing that he was behind her, that he would follow her home.

He did.

She let Dancer out, then flipped off the light switch. As Rick climbed the steps to the porch, she sat down in the swing that hung at one end. He sat at the other end, leaving enough room for another person between them, and he gazed off into the dark.

Every house on the block was dark except for the porch lights and the occasional flood lamp. None of her neighbors lived a nocturnal life, though old Mr. Bennington did have a tendency to get up around one in the morning to sneak a forbidden snack from his wife's kitchen. She fussed at him for doing it, and he fussed back at her for not letting him have sweets during the day. Amanda had never heard a conversation between them where the subject didn't come up, but their marriage was going on sixty-five years. They were doing something right.

Would she have that kind of luck? Would she ever have a marriage at all?

Her gaze slanted toward Rick.

For distraction, she said the first thing that came to her. "Julia told me about you two. Sorry."

He was already distracted. When he turned to her, his expression was puzzled. "What about us?"

"That you'd broken up."

"Oh. Yeah. Thanks."

Oh. Yeah. Thanks? What kind of response was that?

Okay, so Amanda didn't understand his and Julia's relationship. She'd thought that they were a tad unconventional, but apparently there had been less to the relationship than she'd assumed. She just naturally associated *long-term* with love and commitment. Not everyone else did.

Lucky for her, in this case.

Dancer came onto the porch, her steps delicate in spite of her size. She nuzzled Amanda's leg, then sniffed Rick intently before resting her head on his knees, staring up at him with her gorgeous brown eyes. "Geez, dog, why don't you just climb on up in my lap?" he grumbled.

"Don't invite—"

Too late. With one sleek, powerful jump, Dancer bounded onto his lap, turned on the unsteady surface of his thighs, then plopped down, her head leaning against his chest, her lips curled back in what Amanda was sure was a grin.

"You're not a dog person, are you?" she asked as he stared down at forty pounds of puppy.

"Not so you'd notice."

"Dancer, come here," she scolded.

The dog lifted her ears, considered it, then resettled with a heavy sigh.

"She learned to 'come up' very quickly, but there's something about 'get down' that doesn't compute in her brain. Just shove her off."

He did so, pushing Dancer onto the bench between them. The dog rolled onto her back, legs splayed, and rested her head once again on Rick's legs.

"She has no modesty, does she?" he asked drily.

"Of course not. Her mama's a stripper. Didn't you have dogs when you were a kid?"

"Yeah, sure, but they weren't allowed inside the house and they weren't too fond of kids. They always hid when they heard my brothers and me coming."

"Gee, imagine that."

"Aw, we weren't bad kids. At least, not seriously so."

He gave in and began scratching Dancer's belly. Tongue lolling, she gazed up at him with pure puppy admiration. "What about you? Did you have pets?"

"No." A dog was to have been her Christmas present the year she was seven, a beautiful spotted dalmatian. Her mother hadn't wanted a dog and had insisted that if they had to have one, one from the pound would do just as well as some fancy registered breed. But her dad had promised, and he never broke his promises.

At least, not by choice. His accident had been in late October; he'd spent Christmas and Easter and the Fourth of July in the hospital. Even at seven, Amanda had known intuitively that there would be no more talk of a dog.

Her mother had been right about one thing, though: a pound puppy was just as good as a registered dog— even better. Dancer had come from the shelter and she was wonderful.

"Do you like to fish?" she asked, just to break the silence.

"Yeah. My granddad felt it was his duty to teach all of us. Promise him a catch and he would go anywhere in the world."

"There was a river about half a mile from our house. My dad spent more hours on those banks than anyplace else besides work." Fishing had made David happy. Those times that her mother had packed sandwiches and cold lemonade for a picnic while he fished were among her fondest memories. She didn't have many of them, though. After all, she'd been only six when they ended.

"My old man wouldn't touch a fishing pole with... well, a ten-foot pole."

"Is that why you've never gotten married and had kids? Because of the example your father set?"

His gaze was razor sharp in the night, but his tone was mild. "I never said I hadn't been married."

She felt a tinge of…disappointment? He was thirty-six, sexy, with that previously mentioned old Georgia name and money, and he had a grin that could charm a woman right out of her thong. It made sense that he'd been married at least once.

"No, you didn't."

He waited a beat, two, then said, "Though I haven't."

"Afraid of commitment?"

Again with the sharp gaze. "No. Just waiting for the right time. Like you, I've had other priorities in my life."

"Tending bar at a strip club?"

"Hey, strippers don't get to look down on bartenders."

"I've been looked down on enough in my life. I would never judge anyone else by their profession." Dancer, now snoring softly, began to twitch and Amanda reached over to rub her belly. "But isn't your family a little disappointed?"

"They'd be happier if I was back home working in the family business, but that isn't going to happen and they know it. I like my job, I stay out of trouble and I don't ask them for money. Mom says that's all any woman can ask of her child."

Brenda wouldn't agree. Amanda liked her job, stayed out of trouble and gave money to Brenda and Dana when they needed it, but Brenda had wanted so much more.

As she rubbed Dancer's silky black fur, Rick's fingers brushed hers. An accident, she thought the first time. Deliberate, she knew the second. It would be so easy to take his hand, to push Dancer out of the way and close the distance between them. It would be so damn easy to kiss him.

But she didn't. If this were nothing more than a fling, she wouldn't hesitate. But it felt like a whole lot more. It felt like a chance. An opportunity.

Maybe a future.

"I'd better get inside," she said, scooting to the edge of the swing. "It's been a long night and Julia wants one more practice before her audition tomorrow night. Good night."

She went to the door and opened the screen for Dancer, who leaped from the bench with a grunt, then padded into the house.

When Amanda followed, locking both doors behind her, Rick was still sitting on the swing in the dark. She thought about asking him to come in, even if it was too soon. If this was an opportunity for something more, rushing the sex wouldn't change that.

But still, there in the dark hallway, she hesitated. He made the decision for her. His footsteps sounded on the porch, followed by the slam of his car door, then the engine making that beefed-up growl.

As he drove away, she regretted her hesitation. A lot.

Almost Heaven smelled like carpet deodorizer and lemon cleaner when Amanda entered the main room Sunday evening. Whoever had the job of closing during the week did a cursory cleaning job, but on Sunday mornings a professional crew took over. The glass shelves behind the bar gleamed, the lacquered tables were spotless and the chairs were arranged just so around them.

Julia had already arrived and was dressed in booty shorts and a Lycra scarf top that left her shoulders bare and dipped in a vee to her navel. The color was baby blue, a nice complement to her porcelain skin. The only other thing she wore was a pair of four-inch platforms, easier to dance in, and an expression of mixed excitement and trepidation.

"I think I'm going to puke," she murmured as Amanda joined her and Eternity at a table in the middle of the room.

"If you do, be careful not to slip in it," Eternity said with a grin and a sly wink.

"You'll be fine." Amanda patted Julia's arm and found her skin ice-cold. "Once the music starts, just pretend you're back at my house. Relax and go with the flow."

"Easy for you to say. You were both born sexy. I'm trying to fake it."

"Okay, I'm here." Harry's voice boomed through the large room as he came in from the corridor at the far end of the bar that led to his office and the storeroom.

Behind him was Vincent. Eternity made a small face of repulsion. Having experienced more than a few of his come-ons, Amanda knew exactly how she felt.

"You'll be fine, Julia," Amanda said. "We'll be sitting right here—"

"No." Hands fluttering in the air, Julia shook her head vigorously enough to set her hair swaying. "I've changed my mind. You guys wait at the bar, would you? And don't watch?"

Eternity linked her arm through Amanda's. "We'll do whatever you want, girl. Just go up there and have fun." She sent a pointed look Vincent's way, then added, "Knock 'em dead."

Harry took a seat, Vincent started the music and Amanda and Eternity strolled to the bar, keeping their backs to the stage.

"When I first started, the older girls always said don't spend time at the bar," Eternity said, her accent a pleasant accompaniment to the Latin music Julia had chosen. "The men see you standing around doing nothing, they think you're not worth paying for."

"Was that in Jamaica?" Amanda asked.

"Yeah. I was fifteen, helping my mama raise all seven of my brothers and sisters."

"And you're still helping raise someone," Amanda said with a nod toward the stage behind them.

Eternity tapped Amanda's cheek with one long red nail. "Like I haven't watched you play mama hen to the younger girls ever since I came here. Monique, Lisa, Rica, Pilar…"

Three of the four were still at Almost Heaven, but Lisa Howard had quit a few months earlier. She'd been a good dancer but a bad money manager, spending it on clothes and cars and good times when the cash was coming in, bumming a bed to sleep in when it wasn't. She had often talked about going back to school and when she'd quit last August, Amanda had hoped that was the reason. She didn't know, though, because Lisa hadn't said goodbye. One day she didn't show up, and Harry had said—

Harry said she wasn't coming back.

That she'd gotten a better offer.

Despite the long sleeves she wore, a chill danced down Amanda's spine. First Lisa, then DinaBeth, then Tasha. *Haven't you ever wanted to change your life?* she'd asked Rick when they'd talked about DinaBeth and Tasha. But three girls who worked together all acting on that desire within weeks of each other? All three getting better offers, going off to God knew where?

Coincidence? Or something more?

She was staring into the distance, trying to think of any other dancers she knew who had taken off like that recently, when Vincent walked behind the bar and gave them his biggest, oiliest smile.

"What can I do for you pretty ladies?"

Eternity tapped that long red nail again, this time on her own cheek. "Oh, I don't know. Drop dead, maybe?"

He exaggerated a wounded look. "You hurt my feelings, Eternity."

"I've heard that other girls have hurt a lot more than that. What was it? A black eye? A split lip?" Eternity slid a sly glance Amanda's way. "A knee to the groin?"

Vincent shot a venomous look at Amanda, who summoned a smile from the memory. "How many times had I warned you to keep your hands to yourself? I even told you what I was going to do if you ever touched me again. Bright guy that you are, you did, and I did. And I'll do it again if you give me a reason."

Vincent shifted behind the bar, his movements jerky. "You know, bitch, you're not that hot. I can find plenty of girls better than you."

"Yes, but will they let you come near them?" Eternity shook her head with mock sympathy. "I don't think so."

"Screw you both." Vincent sneered. "You don't mean nothin' to me. Snotty little bitches." He stormed away, slamming the door behind him as he disappeared down the back hallway.

Eternity grinned. "What do you think he has on Rosey that Rosey keeps him hanging around?"

"They're related. Vincent's mother and Rosey's mother are cousins."

"Vincent has a mother?" Eternity shuddered at the thought. "It's a good thing for Rosey's family that he's got this business for all the freaks to work in. Chad, the musclebound fireplug, is also related."

"And Derek, the bouncer at the Marietta club." Amanda fell silent. Rick had worked at that club for a while before moving to Almost Heaven. That was where he'd met Tasha, who'd moved on…maybe. Who was friends with DinaBeth, who'd also moved on…maybe. Who hung out with Lisa, who'd also…

"Eternity, were you friendly with Lisa?"

She puckered her glossy browned-down red lips in thought, then shrugged. It was an eloquent gesture that involved her entire body, rippling, artless and sensuous. "I gave her advice sometimes when you weren't around. We went out for drinks a time or two. Why?"

"Did she say anything to you about leaving?"

"No. But it happens, chica. You know that. Most girls aren't in this for a career. They're playing, experimenting, enjoying their power over men. They get married, pregnant, fat, lazy and they move on. And we *are* our own bosses. We don't *have* to give notice."

That was true. Most dancers were self-employed.

Giving notice was a courtesy. But a dancer didn't want to leave a club manager short-handed; odds were good she would run into him at another club sometime in the future.

"But if you were moving on, wouldn't you tell the rest of us? Wouldn't you want to say goodbye?"

"Of course I would."

"Lisa didn't."

Another intricate shrug.

"Neither did DinaBeth. Or Tasha. They all left within two months, and none of them told anyone. They just left." *Disappeared.* It had an ominous sound to it.

Eternity stared at her a moment, then circled the bar and poured herself a shot of rum. She offered the bottle to Amanda, who shook her head, then returned it to its place on the shelf. After tossing down the liquor, she said, "They moved on. It's not unusual. And they didn't say goodbye. Apparently, we didn't matter as much to them as we thought. Oh, well. Now…" She set the glass down and took a deep breath. "Eternity has to retire to the dressing room to make herself beautiful for tonight. Enjoy your evening off."

"Yeah, I will," Amanda murmured. She didn't have any plans for the evening, which meant she would either work on her bedroom or veg out in front of the TV with Dancer. Neither held much appeal.

The music stopped and a low murmur of voices came from across the room. A moment later, Julia appeared beside her, practically jumping out of her skin. "I got the job!" she said with a breathy squeal. "Can you believe it? I did it! Harry said I could dance tonight if I wanted. Not on the main stage, of course, but one of the side stages. Isn't that cool?"

"That's cool," Amanda agreed. "Congratulations."

"Oh my God, look at me! My knees are knocking and my hands won't stop shaking. Delayed reaction, I guess. I've never been so nervous in my life! But Harry said I did well. He said I'll loosen up some as I get experience. Of course I will. I'm so pumped!"

Had she been that excited when she passed her first audition? Amanda wondered with a small smile. Probably. She'd definitely never been so nervous, and *she* was born to be a dancer. For Julia, who'd been born to be a bookkeeper, it must have been incredible.

"I think I will dance tonight," Julia decided. "Will you tell Rick?"

"I won't see him until tomorrow night, if he's working."

"You could call him. Better yet, go by the apartment. I'm sure he's there. You remember how to get there?"

Of course she did. She'd given him a ride home just a few nights ago. But last night she'd come *this* close to opening the door again and asking him to spend the night with her. No way was she going to his apartment, and she wasn't calling him. She wasn't that foolish.

"I think this is something you should tell him."

Julia studied her a moment, then grinned. "Coward."

"I've been called far worse names than that. I'd better go now. Dancer's expecting me back soon since I didn't feed her dinner before I left. Have fun dancing. And congratulations again. I'm proud of you."

Before Amanda could take more than two steps, Julia

enveloped her in a hug. "Thanks," she whispered, then just as quickly let go, turned and headed for the dressing room.

Amanda drove home, CD player silent, thinking about Lisa, DinaBeth, Tasha…and Rick. She looked long and hard at the apartment complex where he lived, but she didn't turn in. Tasha had lived there, too, for a while, then she, DinaBeth and four or five other girls had rented a house a few miles away. A couple of the girls were college students; a couple held nine-to-five office jobs. It was kind of like living in a sorority, Tasha had said, except the house was shabby and they weren't snotty, rich bitches.

Do you think something happened to Tasha? she'd asked Rick.

He did, and now she wondered, too. Coincidences happened, but so did tragedies. Not that many people considered a crime against a stripper a tragedy. The way they dressed, the things they did for money…

Dancing around half-naked in front of strangers, Amanda, you're just asking for trouble. Don't come crying to me when you get it.

She hadn't gone crying to her mother for anything since the day they buried her father.

Functioning on autopilot, she turned into her driveway, shut off the engine and got out of the car. She was across the yard and halfway up the steps, listening to Dancer howl, when she realized she wasn't alone. Rick was stretched out on the porch swing, his jacket wadded into a ball to turn the wooden arm into a pillow. He didn't sit up as she climbed to the porch and turned in his direction, but he did speak.

"Would you please let that dog out? She's been carrying on like that since I got here."

"She's a guard dog. You're trespassing on her property." She unlocked the door and opened the screen just in time to keep Dancer from tearing through it. The puppy bounded across the porch, not to defend her mistress and territory, but to leap onto the swing—making Rick grunt—and make every effort to lick his face.

He held her at arm's length, then finally wrestled her into a position where he could sit up. "Some guard dog. Does she lick intruders to death?"

"Apparently, she's decided she likes you." She shrugged. "She's a puppy. She has frequent lapses in good judgment."

"Aw, you like me, too. Hell, *I* like me, and I never have lapses in good judgment."

Amanda thought it better not to respond to that. Instead, she sat in the nearest chair, resting her purse on her lap, and said, "Julia passed the audition."

"Good."

"She's dancing tonight if you want to go see her."

He shook his head. "I'll see her when I'm getting paid to be there."

She shook her head, too. "None of my boyfriends ever wanted to pay to watch me dance—well, except the one who got turned on watching other guys watch me. They all wanted me to do it for free at home."

"Hey, I paid you nearly four hundred bucks for Julia's lessons. Doesn't that entitle me to one private dance for free?"

"My retirement fund thanks you."

"You're a tough woman."

"I'll take that as a compliment."

"I meant it as a compliment."

Smiling, she gazed across the lawn. It was time to pull up the scraggly remains of the summer flowers and fill the beds with pansies that would stay bright all winter long. Waves of blue, with clumps of yellow here and there, along with a few pots of bronze mums for the porch. They would be a lovely sight to come home to from her new job.

But for five more weeks, she was still doing her old job, and that reminded her again of the three girls. Shifting in the chair so she faced Rick, she asked, "Do you know a dancer named Lisa Howard?"

He was idly scratching Dancer behind the ears, watching the dog make goofy faces instead of looking at her. "I don't think so. Why?"

"She worked at Almost Heaven. She was friendly with Tasha and DinaBeth. She quit unexpectedly about a month before DinaBeth did."

"Girls quit. You said it happens all the time."

"She didn't tell any of us. One day she didn't come in and Harry said she'd gotten a better offer."

If she hadn't been watching so closely, Amanda wouldn't have seen the way his fingers stilled in Dancer's fur for just an instant. Wouldn't have noticed the stiffness when he turned his head to look at her. Wouldn't have felt the change in the air.

Then his fingers started moving again and everything seemed perfectly normal. Just one odd little moment out of time. "Sounds like Harry needs to broaden his vocabulary."

"You don't think it's strange, that Lisa disappeared, then DinaBeth, then Tasha? That they all gave Harry the same excuse?"

"*Disappeared* is a strong word to use. Just because you haven't seen them doesn't mean they've vanished."

"A few days ago you thought Tasha might have gotten into some sort of trouble. Now you act as if it's nothing? No big deal?" She drew a breath and leaned forward. "Tell me, Rick. Do you believe something's happened to Tasha?"

Chapter 7

Rick wished he had resisted the impulse that had brought him to the house to wait for Amanda this evening. He didn't want her to get overly curious about the three dancers and start asking questions. It was one thing if he or Julia inadvertently made Rosey suspicious—they were trained to deal with it—but another entirely if Amanda did. Rosey might be fond of her, but he wouldn't let emotion interfere with activities that could land him in prison. He wouldn't hesitate to make her disappear, as well.

And it would be Rick's fault for rousing her suspicions in the first place.

Grimly he stared at her across the porch. He didn't feel a moment's guilt as he lied. "Yeah, I think it's coincidence. I was just curious, but you convinced me there was no reason to be. They decided to leave the club. Maybe they did have other offers, or maybe they just got tired of Vincent drooling over them. Their families and friends aren't worried. Why should anyone else be?"

"DinaBeth's parents broke off all contact with her when she moved out. Tasha wasn't in touch with her family, either. They probably don't even know their daughters are missing."

"There's no proof they are."

"But—"

"Amanda." He said her name quietly, but the edges were still sharp. "Remember? They may be living happily-ever-after in Buckhead. Or Hollywood. Or two miles down the street, dancing at another club or acting in porn movies or running their own triple-X-rated Web site. There are a thousand more likely explanations than something bad happening to them."

"Maybe," she said grudgingly.

He should have let it drop there, but instead he asked, "What made you suspicious? When we were talking the other night, you were pretty sure everything was on the level."

"The other night I'd forgotten about Lisa. Eternity mentioned her at the audition and I just wondered…"

"They all left in the summer. Popular time for moving on. If they were smart, they headed south and are sitting on a tropical beach drinking piña coladas as we speak."

"Maybe," she repeated, this time not so grudgingly. "So you've noticed Vincent's way with the ladies."

Rick laughed. "I heard one of the dancers kicked him in the balls for grabbing her before a set."

She clasped her hands primly on her lap. "Actually, I kneed him. I didn't kick him until he'd fallen to the floor."

"You?" His brows raised high. He knew she was strong—pole and floor work took some muscle, to say nothing of the jogging and weights to stay in shape—but there was still something delicate about her. She was gentle. He found it hard to imagine her hurting anyone, but if she had to, Vincent was a good choice.

She stood, as fluid and sexy in jeans and a long-sleeved rugby shirt as in her breakaway skirts and bras, and walked to the door. "Let that be a warning to you. Do you want to come in?"

Pushing Dancer aside, he stood, too. "I don't need a warning. If I grab you, you'll like it too much to try the same maneuver. Besides, now I'm forewarned. And, yeah, I'd like to come in. I want to see this bedroom everyone's been talking about."

"I'll give you the grand tour." She held the screen door until he caught it, then turned away, flipping on light switches. "This is the living room."

The colors on the wall were so pale as to barely be there. The wood floor gleamed and the glass tile around the fireplace looked like chunks of ocean water from his last Caribbean dive trip. The furniture was girlie stuff—upholstered, straight lines, not an ounce of comfort in the bunch.

With its brown walls, the dining room–turned–workout room was more to his liking. The home gym could come in handy, and the stripper pole…oh, yeah, that could, too.

The kitchen was cool—very modern with an old oak table that easily could have been in his great-granny's kitchen a lifetime ago. And the bathroom—black and granite with a Jacuzzi tub. Add a flat-panel television high on the wall, and he'd found his favorite room.

Then she led him into the bedroom. Dancer, who'd been trotting along, brushed past and leaped onto the bed, settling into a depression that was roughly her shape. "Awful, isn't it?"

That was a polite description. For starters, the room was dark. Even after she'd turned on all three lamps, it remained dim. She'd stripped the doors and trim, and the nearest wall was down to bare Sheetrock, with clumps of adhesive and occasional scrape marks showing that neither the paper nor the wall had given up easily.

The paper remaining on the other walls may have once been flowers on a tan background, but years had aged the paper and the tan was now a nasty shade of brown and the flowers looking half-past dead.

"I went through brown, white, black and a really interesting shade of turquoise paint to get to bare wood," she commented. "There was a turquoise area rug, too. It was definitely the ugliest thing in the house."

"And you're putting wallpaper back up in here?"

"I'm thinking about it. There are places where the paper refuses to come off without damaging the drywall. New paper will cover that up. Paint means I repair or replace."

"Yeah, but wallpaper. Reminds me of my grandmothers' and my aunts' houses. You know, fussy, prim places." He looked at her, leaning against an oak dresser that showed signs of age. The mirror behind her reflected the straight line of her back, the bend of her elbows, the curve of her fingers as they curled over the edge of the dresser on each side of her hips. And her hips… Thank God for hips.

"Well, God forbid that I come off as a prim, fussy person. But repairing drywall does tip the scale in that direction."

"My brother, Russ, can show you how."

She waved him away. "I know how. I've stripped paper from every room in this house. It's just tedious. So is mudding and taping new drywall. That's why I'm leaning toward wallpaper."

"Pricey wallpaper."

"Hmm. Pale stripes with a wisteria border. I love wisteria. There was a huge vine growing in the oak beside our house when I was a kid and while they were in bloom they were the first thing I saw when I woke up."

Rick got the impression she didn't have too many pleasant childhood memories to draw on. Growing up poor, then having her father's devastating accident. He hoped the company Mr. Nelson had worked for had done right by him and his family, but it didn't sound as if they had.

Finally, he moved farther into the room, going to lean against the dresser at the opposite end. As he turned, he saw a faded photograph tucked into the corner between the mirror and its frame. He pulled it loose and studied it. A sunny day, a pretty woman, a nice-looking guy, the woman holding a Bible in the crook of her arm. On the other side of the man, holding his hand, was Amanda. There was no mistaking those copper curls. She wore a sundress printed with bright flowers, sandals with a matching flower centered on each one and a straw hat with a matching band and flower. Her hair, barely reaching her shoulders, corkscrewed out from under the hat every which way.

"Look at that sweet face," he teased. "How could they not want three or four just like you?"

"Sweet faces can be deceiving. Look at your mother. She saw you and had two more and *then* found what she was in for."

"But she loves us all dearly." For an instant, Amanda went still and Rick could have kicked himself. Why not just rub her face in the fact that her mother didn't love her dearly?

The moment passed and Amanda straightened, moving toward the door. "I'd invite you to stay for dinner, but all I have in the refrigerator is fat-free yogurt, carrots, celery and salad greens."

"You were planning on a rabbit dropping by?" He replaced the photo where he'd found it, then followed her out. "I've got something better in my car. I went home to see Mom today and she packed leftovers. Want to share?"

"Sure." But her tone was less than enthusiastic and her smile was faint, uncertain.

Rick chose to ignore those signs. He went out to his car, retrieved the cooler from the trunk, then carried it into the kitchen. He began unpacking neatly arranged storage containers, reading out their contents. "Ham with a maple glaze, some sort of proscuitto and asparagus thing, potato salad, baked beans, pulled chicken with mustard sauce, tabouli, corn salsa, some of my aunt Jo's bread-and-butter pickles, cornbread, dinner rolls, crab claws—shells already discarded—and dessert. Poppy seed cake, Grandma's chocolate cake with caramel icing and oatmeal cookies."

Amanda was staring at the array of food. "Does she feed you like this all the time?"

"It was some sort of family thing today. A cousin's kid's birthday. Everyone brought food. My family has great cooks." Or, in a few instances, they hired great cooks.

She set two of everything on the counter—plates, glasses, silverware, napkins—then filled the glasses with tea. Instead of trying to make do at the oak table not quite big enough for two, they loaded the plates and went to a wicker table on the back porch.

They ate silently for a while, then she paused with a forkful of poppy seed cake in midair. "I can't remember the last time I saw my mother."

He didn't know what to say. *I'm sorry? She's an idiot? You're better off without her?*

With a tight little smile and a tighter little shrug, she said, "I'm not saying that for sympathy or anything. I've accepted that she wants nothing to do with me as long as I'm dancing. But I just really can't remember the last time I saw her. We talked for a few minutes on Mother's Day. She said the flowers were pretty. I said good. We talked on her birthday and at Christmas and on Thanksgiving, but I can't remember…" Her voice trailed off into the quiet evening and her gaze followed.

Rick took one last bite of caramel-iced cake, then pushed the plate away. If he hadn't already been full, he would have lost his appetite anyway. "Are you going to tell her when you change jobs?"

Amanda glanced at him. "Sure."

"What if it makes a difference to her? What if she's willing to acknowledge a daughter who's a college instructor? If she wants to be Mom again."

"She probably will."

"Will you let her?"

"Maybe. Probably. But we'll never be close. She'll always remember that I spent twelve years being a bad and shameful daughter, and I'll never forget that for twelve years, she treated me like I wasn't good enough or pure enough to be in her presence." She mashed the rest of the cake together, then licked the cream cheese frosting from the fork. "But she's my mother. It's not much, but you work with what you've got."

Rick started shaking his head before she finished. "If my old man was still alive, I wouldn't have a damn thing to do with him. He wasn't there for us; why the hell should we be there for him?"

"If that's really how you feel, then that's fine. I know my mother and I are never going to have a normal mother-daughter relationship. I'm not sure we ever did. She preferred Daddy and so did I. He was the bond that held us together. Once he was gone, it was really no surprise that she and I couldn't stay together. But he loved her and I did, too, and if we can manage some type of mutually respectful friendship, out of respect to him, then I'd like that."

Rick's laughter was dry. "Go ahead. Make me feel like a spiteful kid."

"There's nothing wrong with your feelings. Ask me again in six months and I might feel the same. Some people are just difficult. Your father was one of them.

My mother is, too, and so is my aunt, her best friend. Dana has a lot of influence on what Mom does and thinks, and even if Mom is willing to have me back in her life, Dana might not be."

"It'll be their loss. It's been their loss."

She looked surprised, then smiled faintly. "Thank you."

"Let's clean up here and go for a ride," he suggested, wanting to lighten the mood. "We'll put the top down and enjoy the pollution over Atlanta. Come on, we'll even take Dancer with us."

"Dancer gets carsick. When she goes to the vet, she has to sit in the front seat and she still pukes sometimes."

"Okay, we'll leave Dancer tucked in for the evening. It'll be just you and me." Without waiting for a definite yes, he stood, gathered their dishes and went inside. She brought up the rear with their glasses and the tea pitcher. While he packed the food back into its containers, then into the cooler, she rinsed the dishes, loaded the dishwasher and set out a metal plate with Dancer's supper. Before the dish touched the floor, the dog came racing in from the bedroom.

Less than ten minutes after he'd made the suggestion, he was lowering the top on the Camaro, then sliding into the driver's seat beside Amanda. She sat primly, feet together, hands folded. All she needed was to cross her arms over her chest for classic closed-off body posture.

"I'm restoring the car myself," he said as he pulled away from the curb. "I'm about to start on the exterior."

"You don't like primer gray paint?"

"She's gonna be red when I'm done. With black leather interior."

"Sounds flashy."

"I like flashy."

"Most boys do." Digging into her purse, she pulled out a thick band and twisted her hair into a ponytail, wrapping the band over and around three times, catching the ends the third time to keep them from blowing. Then she leaned her head back and lifted her gaze to the night sky.

He did exactly what he'd suggested: drove aimlessly along the surface streets until they came to the on-ramp for northbound I-85. Once on the freeway, he kicked up the speed to five miles over the limit. It created too much wind to talk, but he didn't care. He was driving down the highway on a cool Georgia night with a beautiful woman who made him hot. Who needed talk?

He did—rather, a good talking-to. He was taking a big risk spending time with her, getting involved with her. He could compromise his case. He could compromise his and Julia's safety. If Amanda turned out to be part of Rosey's illegal operations, he could lose his job. And yet instead of turning around and heading straight back to her house, he exited the interstate onto a two-lane highway. Instead of then hightailing back to his apartment, he followed the road into a heavily wooded area and turned onto a gravel road.

No Fishing After 7:00 p.m. the sign at the open gate read, but he ignored it and followed the climbing road to its end, then cut the engine.

They were at the top of the hill, an old mill pond just below them, the city of Atlanta and its suburbs spread beyond that. During the day it was just houses, cars, buildings and people for as far as you could see, but at night, with millions of lights twinkling, it was impressive.

"Is this one of your fishing holes?"

"Yeah. Though I prefer the river back home."

"Why did you bring me here?"

He dragged his fingers through his hair. "I don't know. Maybe to kiss you."

"You could have done that at my house."

That was a jolt to his system. Of course, he'd known he could persuade her, but to hear her admit that she was willing… "But if we'd done it at your house, it wouldn't have ended with one kiss."

"No," she agreed, her voice a sweet murmur.

"And I'm not sure I can handle anything more right now."

She nodded. "You have priorities."

"So do you."

She nodded again. "And you need time to get used to not being with Julia."

Not hardly. But he wasn't about to tell her that he'd never *been* with Julia, because she would want to know why they'd pretended and he couldn't tell her. Or she would think he'd just been using Julia until someone else came along and that wasn't true, either. So he sat there, biting his tongue, and let her think he was recovering. Let her think it was too soon for him when he'd already forgotten every woman before Amanda and was past the point of wanting her until it hurt.

"I've never been involved with anyone at the club," she said. "Not in twelve years."

"Quite a record." Neither had he, though his stint could be measured in weeks rather than years. No fraternization was supposedly the rule everywhere, but everyone ignored it when the urge hit. Everyone but Amanda. She'd disappointed a hell of a lot of guys in twelve years.

"But there's no rush." She twisted her head to look at him. "If we feel this way now, odds are we'll still feel this way in a few months, right? If you don't hook up with someone in the meantime."

Since the mere sight of her could make him *feel this way*, he figured it was safe to say that wasn't about to change. His hooking up with someone else wasn't likely, either. The problem was, he didn't know if this case would be resolved within a few months. He already had nearly three months of undercover work in on it. It could end tomorrow or six months from tomorrow. There was no way to predict it.

"Yeah," he agreed. "In a few months…"

"When I'm settled in my new job and you've done whatever it is you need to do." She smiled, looking so beautiful and sounding so adult and sensible, when he was feeling frustrated and juvenile.

Then, in a movement so swift and smooth that he never saw it coming, she unhooked her seat belt, leaned across the console, cupped his face in her palms and kissed him. Hard. Hungry.

Her kiss was like her dances—instinctive, teasing, provocative, sensual, sexy, liquid, hot. And innocent. And sweet. She took his breath, raised his temperature, made him hard, made him *hurt*—for sex, for her, for more. All with one kiss and her slender, gentle hands cupping his face.

She stopped and he groaned in protest, reaching for her. Delicately she pushed his hands away, sank back into her seat and fastened the belt. He was dying, damn it, and she was sitting there looking so...

Not smug or complacent. Like she was dying, too. Her features were strained, her breathing faster than usual, shallower, and she raised one unsteady hand to touch her mouth.

This was best, he reminded himself as he started the engine. He was on the job. She didn't have a clue what he really did for a living, who he really was.

It was definitely best for the case, he told himself as he drove back to her house, the silence heavy between them. What if he got intimate with her and then had to arrest her?

Got intimate? the voice in his head sneered. They might not have had sex, but they'd been intimate. Everything about her, about being with her, was intimate.

It was probably best for her, too, he insisted to himself as he pulled into her driveway. She was starting a new life. Respectability was important to her. What were the odds she'd want a bartender at her old strip club being part of it? And if the case was wrapped up by then and he could be honest with her about his GBI job, what were the odds she'd want to continue something begun with a guy who'd lied to her from day one?

She sat there a moment, not looking at him, which he could tell even though he wasn't looking at her. The car engine rumbled like not-too-distant thunder and

Dancer's barks sounded muted through the closed-up house. After a time, she moved to get out. "You should take your cooler."

No, he shouldn't. He should drive away like a bat out of hell the instant she'd cleared the car. But he shut off the engine and climbed out. He might be a fool, but he wasn't leaving Grandma's caramel-iced chocolate cake behind.

He held the screen door while she unlocked the door. She opened it carefully, ready for Dancer to come galloping out, but there was no sign of the mutt. "Uh-oh."

His first instinct was to reach for the pistol holstered in the small of his back, but then she took a step inside and he saw the reason for her comment. A few bits of maple-glazed ham. Some spears of asparagus, though the proscuitto that had wrapped around them was gone. A pile of tabouli, another pile of bread-and-butter pickles, both deemed inedible, apparently. A puddle of mustard-based barbecue sauce, but no chicken.

"Dancer?" Amanda called. Picking her way through the mess, she went straight to her bedroom, throwing back the covers, kneeling so she could see under the bed. "You've been a bad girl, haven't you?"

Her entire body quivering, the dog crept out a few inches at a time. The hair around her mouth was matted with barbecue sauce, maple glaze and caramel icing; her belly was distended.

"Come on," Amanda said. "You go out, then I'll clean you up."

Relieved to not be in trouble, the dog waddled behind her to the back door. There was more mess in the kitchen, where he had stupidly left the cooler sitting on the floor, latched then, unlatched now. "How did she—"

"She's a smart girl. She's trying to learn how to open doorknobs. I think she'll have it figured out before long." Unruffled, Amanda pulled off a length of paper towel and picked up a spray bottle of cleaner. "I'll replace your mother's storage dishes, but I can't do anything about the food. I'm not that good a cook."

"Don't worry. Mom will always cook more and those dishes were the throwaway kind anyway. I'll help you clean."

"No. Thank you." Her smile flashed, quickly there, quickly gone, not reaching her eyes. "Just go on home, would you?"

He didn't want to. He wanted to help pick up the food and the bits of plastic that were all that remained of his mother's dinner. He wanted to mop the wood floor and help clean Dancer's fur. He wanted to stay.

And that was why he had to leave. "Yeah. That's probably best."

He walked out before he could change his mind.

Or lose it.

Monday evening Rick took the night off.

Tuesday, half an hour after opening, Harry sent him to fill in at one of Rosey's other clubs.

Wednesday, Amanda was kept so busy with customers that she hardly had a chance to look at him, much less speak to him.

By Thursday she was missing him and by Friday she decided to do something about it. If he were any other man, she wouldn't worry how to approach him. She would be seductive, would make him a sensual offer that his body couldn't refuse.

And if he were any other man, when it was done, it would be done. No future to keep in mind. No feelings to worry about—neither his nor hers.

But this was Rick. He was special.

She got to the club forty-five minutes before opening, leaving herself plenty of time for clothes and makeup and a visit to the bar while no one else was around. Even if she couldn't think of the words right now, they would come. When she saw him, she would know what to say.

Or—she recalled that kiss Sunday night—she would know what to do.

Julia was already in the dressing room, wearing the prim—from the front, at least—navy dress that she'd bought on their first shopping trip. It had a high neck, a collar and buttons from top to bottom, along with short little sleeves. The kicker was the back of the dress: there wasn't one to speak of. Maybe four inches of fabric that covered her butt and a red G-string. Because the dress didn't allow for a bra, underneath it she wore adhesive bra cups, also in red.

She was going to be out there closer to naked than Amanda had been in six or eight years. Oh, how the straitlaced had fallen.

Amanda greeted everyone, then stepped behind the screen to change. She tugged on a tiny aqua bra, little more than strings with a couple triangles of fabric, then a matching thong. She usually stuck with the Brazilian thongs for the additional coverage, but tonight she went with a T-back thong, as daring as she ever got.

Over those pieces went a matching fishnet top with three-quarter sleeves; it was just long enough to cover her bra. The fishnet shorts were tiny, only a shade bigger than the thong. With six-inch spike heels that had clear straps with a narrow aqua strip running across her foot and her hair pulled back from her face with shell-shaped combs, she was ready to take on any audience.

Including an audience of one.

When she came out from behind the screen, Eternity murmured. "It is the goddess of the sea."

Julia gave her a wide-eyed look. "Wow. I've taken up yoga. Tomorrow I start running. You look great."

"Thanks." Amanda slid into her seat to touch up her makeup. As she dusted shimmery shadow over her lids, she noticed a photograph in Julia's hand. "What's that?"

"I was changing lockers because the door on mine kept getting stuck, and I found this inside the new one. Monique and Eternity were telling me about them." Julia held it out so Amanda could see.

Lisa, Tasha and DinaBeth.

"I told her they got new jobs, new lives," Eternity said. "Just as you're going to have a new life soon. One of these days we'll be calling you Dr. Nelson."

"If you're not ashamed to admit that you know us," Monique added.

"I would never be ashamed of anyone here." Amanda switched the eyeshadow brush for the blush brush. "Well, besides Vincent."

There was a moment of scornful laughter, then Rica said, "Even Vincent's mama is ashamed to admit she knows him. She should have done the world a favor and drowned him at birth."

Julia turned her attention back to the picture. "These girls are just babies."

"You grow up fast in this business." And Rica knew. She was barely twenty-one herself. "Look how quickly it's changed you. Five days ago you were scared spitless at the thought of going onstage and talking to the customers. Now look at you."

"This one may have been a good girl," Eternity said, patting Julia's shoulder. "But she longed to be bad. At the rate you're going, you'll be the most popular one here after Amanda retires."

Tuning them out, Amanda finished her makeup with a touch of bronzer, repositioned the combs that held her hair back from her face, then started to rise from the chair.

She couldn't do it. The knot in her stomach was too heavy, the breath in her lungs too thin. What if Rick said no? He'd been quick to agree that this wasn't a good time for either of them. He hadn't pressed the issue—hadn't kissed her back when she'd stopped kissing him, hadn't given even a hint that he'd like to stay when he'd taken her home. Whatever made this the wrong time for him, he might reject her. While she was quite good dealing with rejection—being a dancer, being her mother's daughter, how could she not be?—there was no sense in going looking for it when she had to be onstage soon, upbeat and smiling.

She would wait until the club closed. This time she

could be the one waiting in the parking lot. She would invite him over for coffee, pop, great sex.

The seven o'clock dancers went onstage and the girls trickled into the main room, Amanda with them. Several of her regulars were there, waiting their turn with her. Some of them had a bit of an ick factor, but for the most part, they were nice guys. They never tried anything inappropriate.

If she ever got married, Amanda vowed, she would never give her husband reason to go seeking attention elsewhere. Simple companionship, someone showing interest in them—that was all most of these guys wanted.

Her first set was at eight. She remembered to smile, to make eye contact when she could, and she kept her gaze from straying to the bar too often. Rick was usually busy when she did look; a time or two, he'd stood back against the wall, arms crossed over his chest, face in shadow. He wore a white button-down shirt tonight, the sleeves rolled up, the color made bright by his dark skin.

If she could persuade him—seduce him—she would undo those buttons one at a time, slowly, caressing and kissing him, making him hot and eager and about to crawl out of his skin. Then she would start on his jeans—

A voice separated from the background noise, slicing through the music. "Hey, it's Mandy. Any of you guys remember Randy Mandy?"

Her steps faltered and she stopped and scanned the audience before catching herself, falling back into the rhythm of the music. That knot in her stomach had tripled, making her movements sluggish. She gripped the pole with both hands for support, swayed side to side, letting her head fall back, her eyes drooping practically shut. Her spine was arched so far that she was at risk of popping out of her bra, but her covert look at the first few rows, albeit upside-down from her angle, showed no familiar faces, no one unusually interested in her.

Maybe she'd misunderstood the shout. Maybe the emotional state she had worked herself into over Rick made her more susceptible to a bad memory from the past. She hadn't heard that hated nickname in fifteen years. It was just a confidence issue that she thought she'd heard it tonight.

She finished her set without incident and went into the dressing room. A couple of girls were changing for their next sets. They nodded, and she nodded back as she snagged a cheap white bath towel from the basket next to the door and blotted the sweat from her face.

Randy Mandy was gone—had never truly existed except in the spiteful form of Robbie Calloway. She'd never understood why he'd chosen her to hurt, what she'd done to deserve what he did.

She *hadn't* deserved it. She'd been an easy target, that was all. As for why he'd chosen her…society always wanted rational explanations for people's behavior, her psychology professor had taught, and such explanations could usually be found. But sometimes people were just mean. Not psychotic or sociopathic; not suffering from post-traumatic stress disorder or cripplingly low self-esteem. They just did mean things, especially kids.

Dropping the towel into the hamper, she pulled the fishnet top and shorts on again. Normally she went into the audience in bra and thong, but tonight she needed more, no matter how flimsy. The illusion of clothing gave her the illusion of coverage.

After inhaling half a bottle of water and reapplying her lipstick, she drew a deep breath, then returned to the main room. Julia was onstage now with Monique and Halle, and Rick was busy at the bar, scowling fiercely. Amanda took another breath, pasted her smile on and plunged into the mass of tables and customers.

It was the usual routine—smile, eye contact, the offer of money. She sat for fifteen minutes, listening, talking, and the knot in her stomach began to dissolve. Another few smiles and looks, and another offer.

An auditory hallucination. She'd never had one before, but there was a first time for everything. That was all it was.

As she was leaving her second customer, a young man suddenly appeared in front of her. He was about her age, dressed in casual but expensive clothes and grinning from ear to ear, a sparkling testament to good orthodontia. "Hi. Uh, hello. Amanda, right? I'm Shawn. No last names, right?" He had a nice, refined Georgia accent, though his voice was less than steady. "How's this— This is how it works, right? I give you money and you come to my table?"

He shoved a handful of bills at her, and she caught a glimpse of two fifties and at least three hundreds. It disappeared into her palm as she smiled. Bless young people with more money than sense. "That works fine. Where's your table?"

"Over here." He started to take her arm, then drew back. "No touching, right? I mean, you could touch me, but I can't touch you, right?"

"Yes, that's how it works. Is this your first night at a club?"

"In a long time and, frankly, I got so drunk the other times that I don't really remember anything about them. Here we are."

It was a table built for five; they numbered seven. As one appropriated a chair for her, the others scooted their chairs around until they were seated, as Monique liked to say, butt to cheek. She wiggled into her chair—no quick escape from this table—and surveyed her customers. All young men, though the one directly across from her looked ten years older, and he wasn't having nearly as good a time. A few of the faces seemed vaguely familiar, but that was no cause for concern in this business. Along with their regulars, there were new men in the club every night of the week.

She gave her name and each man around the table offered his. The morose man was named Tom and he was the reason for their being at Almost Heaven. He was getting married the following weekend. Bet he'd had no say in how they celebrated the end of his freedom.

"Looks like you've lost a friend," she said, nodding toward the empty seat beside her.

"Nah. He'll be back. In fact, here he comes."

She turned to look, but another customer blocked her view until the man put his hands on the backs of his own chair and the one to its right, swung through the narrow opening and dropped into the seat. He wore a ready grin, along with a haze of too much alcohol in his blue eyes and the fragrance of eau de booze.

"Hey, Mandy. Long time no see. Guys, this is the one, the only, Randy Mandy."

Her breath froze in her lungs. Robbie Calloway, in the detested but living flesh. In *her* club. Talking to *her.* With the exception of her long-ago dream that she'd done her whole stripper routine on the stage at the Copper Lake Baptist Church, Robbie invading her turf like this was the worst thing she could imagine.

"What's the matter, Randy Mandy? Cat got your tongue? We used to figure that family of yours ate cats, you know, being that you were so poor." He looked around the table for encouragement and got it from most of the others. Tom just looked as if his evening couldn't get much worse.

Join the club.

Robbie grabbed her arm, and while she tensed, she didn't pull it away. Shawn intervened for her. "Hey, Robbie, you can't touch her. It's against the rules."

"Screw the rules. My brother works here and his rules are that no one messes with his little brother."

Did Rick know Robbie was here? Was he watching from the bar at that very moment? Had Robbie already told him everything he knew about Amanda? Except the truth. Robbie'd never told anyone the truth.

She twisted in her chair, trying to get a clear view of the bar. Vincent was working at the nearest end. She couldn't see the other end.

It was all right. Chad was just around the corner at the front door. She had regular customers who felt a little proprietary toward her, some a little paternal, scattered through the crowd. The other girls were all around, and she had no doubt every one of them would come to her aid if she screamed.

The panic wasn't for her safety now. It was all that long-ago pain. That humiliation. She'd had little enough pride when she was fifteen in Copper Lake; Robbie had stolen every bit of it for his own amusement, nothing more.

Straightening her spine, she looked at each man in turn except Robbie. "You guys could use better taste in choosing your drinking partners."

"Oh, yeah, like people are going to take advice from you. Town whore of Copper Lake. She slept with half the guys in our class."

She leaned close to him. "I didn't sleep with any of them, including you. Especially you. You lied, because everyone else was getting laid that summer except you. You were so afraid of being left behind, so afraid of your little secret getting out."

His eyes darkened, filling with rage, and he stood. His chair fell back to the floor and he yanked her from her chair, then kicked it back, too. His fingers were tight around her upper arms, grinding the pattern of the fishnet against her skin. "You were so damn easy. So desperate for attention, living in that dump with your father the cripple and your mother, who scrubbed toilets for my mother. A lying little bitch whore—that's all you were. You thought I really wanted to be friends with you. Like a Calloway would want to be friends with a white-trash Nelson. You were stupid. You were—"

Abruptly a big, tanned hand circled the back of Robbie's neck, squeezing until white spots appeared.

"Get your hands off her now," Rick said, his voice little more than a whisper.

Robbie's slimy smile faltered. "Okay, sure. I imagine she costs a whole lot more today than a few lunches and a couple compliments." He let go and raised both hands in the air. "She wants more money, I got it."

"Shut up." Rick's words were sharp, icy. "Go on, Amanda. Go back to the dressing room."

Before she could move, Robbie made a move toward her. "If she's not staying, we want our money back."

Rick's face took on a crimson tinge, his breathing slow and shallow. His fingers tightened around Robbie's neck enough to make him wince. "That's up to her."

She still clenched it in her palm. From the instant she'd recognized Robbie, she hadn't intended to keep it. Give it to the other girls, buy drinks for everyone on the house, but no way she was taking Robbie Calloway's money home with her.

Her fingers trembling, she opened them, and the bills fell from her sticky palm to the tabletop. Before Robbie could reach for them, Rick gathered them up and handed them to the disapproving Tom. "I'm sure the church can put that to better use than these guys will. Consider it yours if you get them out of here before I throw them out."

Amanda wriggled between the crowded chairs and was weaving her way toward the stage door when Robbie called, "I'll see you again, Randy Mandy. You can bet on that."

What followed was a familiar sound to anyone who'd spent twelve years in clubs: a fist smacking into a jaw, a grunt, chairs scraping, customers scattering, a table breaking. She didn't look over her shoulder, but kept walking, barely able to keep her balance in her six-inch stilettos.

Footsteps sounded behind her once she'd reached the hall—not the solid thud of Rick's boots, but the click of heels along with the softer pad of platforms. Julia and Eternity followed her into the dressing room, where Eternity closed the door for the first time in Amanda's memory. "You okay, sweetie?"

Amanda looked at the red finger marks on both arms, reflected in the mirror, then grabbed a baby wipe from the carton on the counter. "I'm fine," she said, scrubbing the marks. She threw that wipe away, then used another to remove her makeup. "But I'm done for the night."

"Why didn't you knee him in the balls?" Julia asked.

Amanda smiled faintly at the idea. "I couldn't think."

"Probably couldn't have found 'em anyway," Eternity said scornfully. "Has to get drunk and surround himself with friends to find the courage to pick on one woman half his size. He ain't no man."

Julia slid her arm around Amanda's shoulders as she finished removing her makeup. "You probably shouldn't go home alone. Wait here until I clear it with Harry and I'll go with you, okay?"

Amanda patted Julia's hands. "I'll be all right. Really. Friday-night money's too good to skip out on. I'll curl up with Dancer and we'll enjoy some television."

She pulled a dress from her locker, a simple sheath that ran from her neck to the top of her kneecaps. Its stretchy fabric allowed her to pull it on over her head, and its white shade went well with the sleeves of the aqua fishnet top she still wore. "Tell Harry I'm sorry and I'll be back tomorrow."

"We'll walk you to the door," Eternity said and Julia nodded.

They did, standing together on the stoop while she crossed the parking lot to her car. They stayed until she was inside, doors locked, and waved when she drove past. Her own phony smile lasted about halfway home, when she remembered to let it go.

In her driveway, realizing she still wore the six-inch heels, she took them off, then padded barefoot across the cool grass to the warmer steps. She unlocked the door and let Dancer out, watching her for a moment, before calling her back in.

It wasn't even nine o'clock. The last time she'd been home from work this early was when she'd caught the flu and had thrown up onstage. For days, everyone kept asking if she was all right; customers who'd usually taken the stage-side seats moved back a row for weeks.

Ignoring the chaise, she curled into the lone chair in the room. It was hardly comfortable for one, and didn't cut it when Dancer joined her. Still, she needed the contact with the dog. It made her feel better.

By now Rick had talked with Robbie. He knew her old nickname, knew she'd once thought a Calloway cared for her. He'd heard Robbie's claim that she'd slept with him and everyone else and he probably wouldn't even ask if it was true.

She'd lost her virginity at nineteen. She'd experienced the pain, the bleeding, everything associated with the first time.

And right now Rick was thinking of her as Randy Mandy, town whore.

She didn't cry over things like this, not anymore, or she would surely dissolve into a puddle right there.

The television drowned out the sounds of traffic outside, so when the doorbell rang, it caught her by surprise. She looked that way, still curled with Dancer. Julia? Eternity? Rick? Robbie?

"Come on, Dancer," she murmured, switching off the television, pushing to her feet. She curled her fingers around the dog's collar and went to the door, quietly securing the chain lock before undoing the dead bolt. Opening the door three inches, she saw only Rick, and he looked concerned. Not angry. Not disgusted. Not even annoyed with her for lying. It was just concern verging on panic.

He dragged his fingers through his hair. "Can I come in?"

She undid the chain and stepped back. The moment he stepped through the door, Dancer lunged for him, forcing her to release the collar and take a step back, giving them room for their greeting.

Finally Rick met her gaze. "My brother's an idiot."

"Yeah, I noticed he lacks your charm."

"He lacks a functioning brain." Then… "Are you okay? Did he hurt you?"

He meant physical pain, not emotional. "I'll have a few bruises, but that's nothing new."

"So will he," Rick added drily, reminding her of the punch she'd walked out on. "Our mom raised him to be a whole lot better than that, but…" He stepped into the living room doorway, his back to her, then glanced over his shoulder. "Did you know my mom?"

Shivers slid through her, and the knot settled in her stomach again. "I knew who she was. We weren't exactly in the same social group."

"Your dad worked for our logging company. It was *our* truck that lost its load. The accident was our responsibility."

She didn't say anything.

"Did they take care of him?"

"We got some money—insurance, disability, something else. I was six years old. I don't know exactly what he was paid. Just that it wasn't enough. My mother worked two, sometimes three, jobs to make ends meet, and from the time I was able, I picked up the slack from the home health people in caring for my dad."

Slowly Rick turned, his gaze level, giving nothing away. "How did you hook up with Robbie?"

She sighed. From the moment she'd recognized Robbie, she'd known this moment was coming. She didn't know what to tell him but the truth. Quickly.

Moving toward him, she gestured into the living room. "Let's sit down."

Chapter 8

She chose the chair, leaving Rick with the one-armed sofa and Dancer. Digging his fingers into the dog's fur, moving them only minimally, helped him ignore the pain from the scrapes across his knuckles. It had been so long since he'd punched one of his brothers that he'd forgotten how damn hardheaded they were.

Amanda looked about ten years old in that white jumper and pale blue see-through top. But there was nothing girlish about her bare feet—like the rest of her, they were incredibly sexy, even though he'd never had a foot fetish in his life. Her back was straight, her hands clasped together on her lap.

"When I was fifteen, Mom and I decided to switch off. She quit her third job and I got a summer job at the lumberyard, clerking and stocking shelves for your uncle Garry. Robbie worked there, too, more or less."

Rick understood the "more or less." Robbie had known since he was little that there would always be money for him, some family money, some in his personal trust fund, so he'd always done most of his jobs more or less. Why exert himself to earn money for a forty-thousand-dollar car when the family would fund it for him?

"We were the only two young people working there and we became friendly." She looked up, meeting his gaze evenly. "Everything from here on is my version. Any variations from what Robbie's told you, you'll have to figure out on your own."

He nodded once.

"I always took my lunch to work to save money. Robbie started bringing his, too, and we'd walk to the creek out behind the lumberyard. We ate, but mostly we talked—about school and life, what we wanted to do, what our parents wanted us to do. He was friendly and he listened as if what I said really mattered."

An odd expression crossed her face and Rick wondered if she'd made a connection between that and the listening she did for money at work. Not that it was the same. The customers at the club realized it was a business transaction. They didn't mistake her attention for personal attraction.

"As the summer went on, we got pretty close. We went from talking to kissing and making out and, uh, discussing having sex. He was willing, but I wanted to wait for school to start. He called me his girlfriend, but I never saw him outside of work. He never took me on a date. He never gave me a ride home after work. He never called me to talk. I wanted more. I wanted…"

"Acknowledgment," Rick said quietly. As she'd mentioned, they belonged to different social classes. Robbie was sweet-talking and coming on to her in private, but she wanted him to do it publicly. She wanted his friends to see them and know they were together, wanted his family to see them.

That never would have happened. Even if Robbie had genuinely cared for her, he'd been too status conscious. He'd dated cheerleaders and prom queens, not the north side daughter of a paralyzed man and his worked-to-the-bones wife. Amanda had actually worked for money needed to support her family—and knowing Uncle Garry, she'd earned every penny and then some. Robbie had never a dated a woman who actually held a job until he was twenty-seven and out of law school.

"I got acknowledgment, all right," Amanda went on. "Some of his friends had seen us together out by the creek. They saw us holding hands, saw Robbie kiss me. On the first day of school, they started teasing him about it, and he told them that it had just been about sex.

"His girlfriend, Caroline—cheerleader, beauty queen and class president—wasn't putting out, so he'd used me instead. He told them I was easy, I would do it with anyone, and he started calling me Randy Mandy. They all did. And the guys tried. They'd touch me in the hallway and invite me into the backseat of their cars during lunch. Other guys started claiming I'd had sex with them, too. If my father hadn't died and we hadn't moved away, I don't know what I would have done."

Wasn't that a glowing testament for his kid brother? Calling himself and his brothers the spawn of Satan didn't seem funny now.

"You're a strong woman, Amanda."

Now, after the ugly scene at the club, after relating all the old hurts, *now* her eyes filled with tears. She swiped one away, but another appeared.

"Come here." He held out his hand and Dancer tried to climb onto his lap. He pushed her away as Amanda haltingly crossed the room, then laid her hand in his. He pulled her down across him, her hip nestled against his belly, his arm around her back, her head on his shoulder. His free hand brushed gently over her arm, where pale bruises could be seen through the net fabric. By morning they would be dark and ugly, and he just might have to hunt down Robbie and kick his ass.

"I'm not like Robbie. Or my uncle Garry or my father, or any of the other relatives who give the Calloways a bad name."

"I know," she murmured.

"How long have you known I was one of them?"

"Since the minute you walked into Almost Heaven. For an instant, I considered quitting, but then I realized that was arrogance on my part. You didn't have a clue who I was. You'd never known I existed."

"I *am* six years older," he pointed out. "You were twelve when I left Copper Lake. By the time this happened, I was in my third year of college."

She smiled faintly. "I know. Truthfully, I don't really

remember much about you. I have a few vague recol-
lections of you and Mitch, but Russ and Robbie were a
lot closer to my age."

"I'm sorry. I never thought Robbie would come to the
club. Honest to God, I mentioned the name one lousy
time and I never thought he was paying enough attention to remember." One brief mention in one brief phone
call at three in the morning. And the boy didn't usually
remember entire conversations that took place face-to-
face. But to remember and to actually *come* there, when
he'd known Rick was working undercover. And to get
drunk first…

Robbie had screwed up, but so had Rick. And
Amanda had paid for it.

She nuzzled her cheek against his shoulder. "Yeah,
crap happens. I never thought I'd ever see another
Calloway again. At least I know I'll never see Copper
Lake again."

"I don't know." He removed one of the combs from
her hair, then worked his fingers gently through her
curls, loosening them. "You wouldn't go back even to
meet my mother?"

She laughed, but it was underlaid with real tension.
"Mothers don't like me, remember?"

"I told you, Mom is different. She would never be
less than nice to anyone I brought home."

"Even when your brother's telling her I used to be the
town whore?" she asked drily.

Okay, he was definitely kicking Robbie's ass. And
then his mother would take over and Robbie would
really be in trouble.

"Besides, why would you want to take me home to meet your mother?" Another small laugh, another wave of tension.

Shut up, shut up, the voice in Rick's head was chanting. Remember the case? Remember their agreement? That not acting on this thing between them was best? But he ignored the voice, forgot the case, threw out the agreement and acted instead. "Because my mother always meets the important women in my life."

Amanda's eyes darkened. "Always? That sounds like a lot. Fewer than twenty, more than fifty or somewhere in between?"

"Way fewer than twenty. It's three—and that includes Prudence Charles. She was my algebra tutor our junior year in high school, and she taught me about a whole lot more than numbers. She broke my heart when she ditched me for the president of the math club."

"And the second?"

"Her name was Elizabeth, and we dated in college. We thought about getting married, but she was really into politics and images, and I didn't think I'd make a very good First Husband." When Amanda chuckled, he went on. "You think I'm kidding, don't you? She's been our senator for six years and is rumored to be considering a run for the White House."

"And number three?"

"Julia."

Amanda's expression grew wistful. "I bet your mom liked her a lot."

"Yes, she did."

"Probably hoped you two would get married."

"No, she didn't. Julia and me—it was just never that sort of thing." Their relationship had always been a working one and still was, even though they shared an apartment and he'd seen her in practically less than her birthday suit. If he took pictures of her performance at the club—better yet, videos—he could sell them at work and make a fortune. Blackmail her with them, and he could make a bigger fortune.

"And what about this?" Amanda whispered. "What sort of *thing* is this?"

"I don't know." He swallowed, then brushed his mouth across her forehead. "But I'd like to find out."

"What about your priorities?"

"They've changed." That was the truth. At this moment, for this night, the case was on the back burner. Being with Amanda, chasing away that sadness from her eyes, taking care of her—that was what mattered most now.

For a long time, she was still and silent, no doubt considering his words from every angle, applying reason and logic and—he hoped—emotion to them. He was asking her for more than an affair and he damn well wanted her to agree. They were good together. He just wanted a chance to prove it.

"Okay," she said.

"Okay?" he echoed dumbly.

She eased to her feet, backed away, then curled her fingers over the hem of her dress. With movements as graceful and elegant as any world-class ballerina, she peeled the dress over her head. "Stay," she said firmly,

then started for the bedroom, trailing the dress behind
her by one strap.

The secret to an instant hard-on, he'd discovered that
evening, was Amanda in a damn near nonexistent thong.
Both in the club and again now, the sight forced the
breath from his lungs and sent blood rushing to his
erection, spreading fire along the way.

She sashayed through the arched doorway into the
dining room, then called over her shoulder, "I meant the
dog. Not you."

Still feeling struck dumb, he looked at Dancer, curled
beside him. "Yeah, stay," he ordered, his voice thick
and hoarse.

He followed Amanda through the house and into the
dreary bedroom, which was no longer dreary. The trim
had been painted white, the walls papered and new
lights installed that brightened and softened.

"What do you think of the paper?" she asked, tossing
the dress aside and standing primly, hands clasped, next
to the night table, which held a lamp and three plastic
condom packets.

He didn't spare the room another glance. "Beautiful."
She was amazingly beautiful. Long, lean muscles. Incredible skin. Those curls that could give a man erotic
dreams. Delicate features, womanly hips, legs that went
on forever. Every man who walked in the door at Almost
Heaven knew all that about her.

But he was the only one who could see her like that
here. Who could touch her. Who could kiss her. Who
could die inside her.

Then do it again.

"You're about to have hot sex with the best exotic dancer at Almost Heaven." Her tone was light, her smile unsteady. "Do you have any fantasies?"

He snorted. "Only about a million. And they've got nothing to do with exotic dancers. Just you. Amanda Nelson. Incredibly smart, beautiful, talented, sexy woman."

The smile turned shy and she ducked her head. He closed the distance between them, lifted her chin and gazed into her eyes. "Since the first night we talked, I've wanted to…" He covered her mouth with his and her arms automatically went around his neck. The instant his tongue touched her lips, she opened to him and he stroked inside, thrusting, tasting, teasing.

Her fingers threading through his hair, she moved closer, rubbing against him, and he slid his hands to lift her bottom against him. The feel of nothing but net over soft, silky ass made his erection throb, made the fire inside flare until it licked his skin.

When he started to end the kiss, she whimpered, held his head with both hands and thrust her tongue into his mouth. She was hot, too, her breasts swollen, her nipples hard against his chest.

He cupped his palms to her face, pushed her back and kissed her cheek, her temple, her forehead. "Is any of this stuff breakaway?"

"Just the thong." She sounded as rough and ragged as he felt. Wriggling against him, she pulled the top over her head, discarded the bra and shimmied out of the shorts. Blindly he found the clasps on either side of the thong's narrow triangle, and it fell away, too.

Seeing her naked after weeks of seeing her nearly so was incredible. She was amazingly hard and hot and soft, and, damn it, he still had all of his own clothes on.

"When I was onstage tonight, before—" instead of mentioning Robbie, she shrugged, a delicate full-torso thing that made her skin quiver; even her hips did a little shiver "—I saw you at the back of the bar, leaning against the wall, and I thought that if I got the chance, I would undo these buttons. Very. Very. Slowly." She touched the top button with a red-tipped nail and his heart shifted into overdrive. When she actually unfastened the button and brushed her mouth to the skin there, his knees damn near buckled.

She couldn't breathe. Some distant part of her brain that was still functioning was amazed. She ran. She lifted weights and practiced yoga. She did heavy-duty work around the house and danced onstage in eight-inch heels, but at that moment, standing in her bedroom, she couldn't breathe.

She undid the next button and drew her tongue slowly across Rick's chest. A quick glance showed that his eyes were closed, his features strained, but his mouth quirked into the faintest of smiles. He was so damn gorgeous. So damn special.

He was the kind of guy she could love.

No, not *the kind of*.

The guy.

His breathing was labored and fast and became more so as she opened the next two buttons and slid her hands inside. His chest was lightly furred, muscled, broad, and his skin burned as if with a fever. He was hot for her—literally. The knowledge made her smile.

She reached his jeans. She undid his belt, unfastened the button, slid the zipper slowly to its end, then pulled his shirttail free and pushed it off his arms. It landed on the new area rug, bright white against the muted colors.

Now his jeans. They were faded and snug and concealed a pair of navy blue boxers that didn't conceal much at all.

Rick caught her hands as she stroked his erection. "Let me get my boots...." He toed them off, kicked off his jeans, then bent to remove his socks and an ankle holster. He shot her a quick look as he stuck the Velcro to itself, then laid it on the night table. "Does this bother you?"

She'd never known anyone who carried a gun, at least, that she was aware of. "I've seen where you live."

Wrapping his fingers around her wrist, he pulled her down onto the bed with him. They both pushed at his boxers; they both fumbled with the condom. When he thrust inside her, she gave a long, low groan. He felt long and hard. She felt full. She felt...damn, she felt like crying. No, no. She hadn't cried when things were bad with her mother. She hadn't cried when things got ugly with Robbie. She wasn't going to cry when things were oh, so right with Rick.

Even if one tear did seep out.

He kissed it away, then began moving inside her, an easy ride. She stroked him, caressed him, encouraged him with soft touches and softer sounds, and he teased and tantalized her, nibbling at her lip, suckling her breasts, biting her nipples. The heat built, the tension, the hunger, the pace, until the sounds and smells and sensations of sex were all around them, hoarse and musky and damn near more than she could bear.

And just that quickly, it pushed over the edge. More than she could bear. Her back arched, her heart stopped, her breath strangled in her chest, as need so intense it was pleasurable turned into satisfaction so intense it was painful. She couldn't cry out, couldn't plead, couldn't do anything but react, her muscles taut, her body quivering, her vision fading.

Somewhere in the midst of all that emotion, Rick came, too, straining against her, his breath raspy in her ear. His skin was slick with sweat. So was hers. His heart thundered around them. So did hers.

When his arms wouldn't hold him any longer, he collapsed on top of her and she held him, her touches gentle on skin that still prickled with reaction. Slowly, she started breathing again and her gaze brought him into focus. Dazed, handsome, heartbreakingly intent as he stared back at her. In his dark eyes, she saw surprise, tenderness, something more than affection, something that touched her heart and raised a lump in her throat.

Then he summoned the strength to move off her, to lie on the mattress beside her, still touching head to toe, and he gave her a wicked smile. "Hot sex, you said. God in heaven, if it had gotten any hotter, you would have killed me."

She smiled and pressed her lips to his shoulder. "But what a way to go, huh?"

Feeling wanted, needed, satisfied, loved. That was all she'd ever wanted, wasn't it?

Rick awoke Saturday morning to a warm body snuggled behind him, slow, even breath cooling his shoulder. He hadn't slept enough, but any sleep lost to sex was worth losing. He thought about making love to Amanda again—he was already half aroused—but it wouldn't be that easy, because unless she'd developed a taste for canine treats, that was Dancer stretched out behind him.

He pushed back the covers and sat up. The dog snuffled and resettled right in the middle of the bed. Sleeping there was a habit she'd have to break. In fact, sleeping on the bed at all needed to become a thing of the past. He would buy her one of those fancy dog beds and find a nice corner for her.

He dragged his fingers through his hair. Geez, he was thinking like he was going to be a permanent fixture around there. He and Amanda had something special going. But that didn't automatically translate into permanency. She still didn't know what he really did for a living. She didn't know that he was looking to lock up her boss, with whom she was friendly, and God knew who else at the club.

She still didn't know he was acting a role, and when she found out, she was going to wonder if she'd just been screwed by another Calloway brother.

So he'd have to convince her otherwise.

He located his clothes on the other side of the bed and pulled on his boxers and jeans. After a trip to the bathroom, where he found a new toothbrush on the counter next to the sink, he made himself reasonably presentable, then went looking for Amanda.

He found her in the dining room, wearing a sports bra and leggings that hugged her like a second skin from hip to midcalf. Her hair was pulled back and braided, and she was sitting on the yoga mat, eyes closed, breathing deeply.

"There's cereal in the cabinet and muffins on the counter in the kitchen," she murmured, clasping her hands behind her back, then straightening her arms. Still breathing long and slow, she leaned forward and raised her arms high above her back, her forehead an inch above the floor, then sat up and lowered her arms again.

As she repeated the move, he went to the kitchen. The cereal was low-fat, low-taste, and the milk in the refrigerator was one percent. He chose a muffin instead, whole grain, oatmeal, with chunks of wood for fiber. Man, he was going to have to introduce her to the pleasures of Waffle House for breakfast.

When he returned to the dining room, she was still stretching. He sat down on the weight bench, content to watch her and say nothing. The way she moved was incredible. She was more comfortable in her body than anyone he knew.

He'd been pretty damn comfortable there himself.

At last, she turned on the mat to face him. "How's the muffin?"

"It ain't no pecan waffle, darlin'."

"Don't I know it." Wistfulness crossed her face, then was gone. "I didn't expect you up for a few more hours."

"I wouldn't be except for the suggestive rubbing against my back and the heavy breathing in my ear."

She grinned. "You should feel honored. Dancer loves you."

"Uh-huh. If putting up with Dancer is what it takes to get to be with her mama…"

She came to him, plucking a chunk of the remaining bite of muffin and putting it in her mouth. Foolish woman acted like it tasted good. "Since you didn't boot Dancer out of bed, you can come take a shower with her mama."

He let her pull him to his feet and lead the way to the bathroom. "I'd rather try out that tub."

"Oh, good, I've always thought it had possibilities."

Meaning she hadn't shared it with anyone else? He liked that.

"By the way, I like the bedroom."

She glanced over her shoulder as she turned the water on. "Even the wallpaper?"

"Even the wallpaper." It took a hell of a lot more than fussy wallpaper to threaten his masculinity. And, truthfully, it wasn't that fussy—just stripes and the wisteria border. If a man had to wake up to flowers every morning, wisteria were better than most.

"When did you find time to do all this?"

She stripped off her bra, then pinned her hair on top of her head. "I didn't have anything else to do this week. Julia's lessons were finished and no one was hanging around the parking lot after work to distract me."

He was so distracted that he could hardly think to respond. "So I'm a charming distraction?"

"I don't believe I said charming." She pulled off the leggings and a pair of hot pink bikini panties.

"Last night. You said—" Abruptly he broke off, feeling like an idiot. If she had put last night—at least, part of it—out of her mind, he had no business bringing it up again.

She switched on the Jacuzzi as she matter-of-factly said, "That your brother lacks your charm." She gave him a head-to-toe look and murmured, "And a whole lot more."

Just that look made it harder—pun intended—to get his clothes off, but he managed. They got into the tub together, the water warm enough to steam, the jets relaxing. They stretched out, as much as the tub allowed, facing each other, not talking for a long time.

Finally, she broke the silence. "Why do you carry a gun?"

With half a shrug, he parroted her words back to her. "You've seen where I live."

She smiled, but didn't accept that as an answer.

"I just feel more comfortable with it, working where I work, living where I live. If it makes you feel any better, it's not to threaten or harass or intimidate anybody unless they're already threatening me."

"Isn't it illegal to carry a concealed weapon in a bar?"

"Yes, ma'am, it is."

"Does Harry know you have it?"

Another shrug. "As long as one of us shows up to work the door, one to tend the bar and at least three of you to dance onstage, Harry doesn't care about much of anything else out front."

He touched her breast, half in, half out of the water,

and her nipple hardened instantly. "You are an honest person," he said with a grin. "A rare breed in our business." Darting his gaze back up to hers, he quickly added, "I'm an honest person, too."

"If I had any doubts about that, you wouldn't be here."

"Good," he said.

"Good," she repeated.

After another long, intense look, she shifted to kneel above him, water streaming over her golden skin. "Have you ever made love in a Jacuzzi?"

"No."

"Me, neither. Let's change that." Leaning forward, bringing her breasts temptingly close to his mouth, she took a plastic packet from behind the vase of bath beads in the corner.

Rick couldn't keep from chuckling. "You keep condoms in the bathroom?"

"Of course not," she said with a haughty shake of her head that would have been more effective if her hair had been free to toss. "Just one, conveniently tucked away this morning while you snoozed with another female."

"She doesn't smell nearly as good as you," he said, nuzzling her breast. "And she drools."

"I won't drool," she promised. Then she gave him a lascivious grin. "But I just might howl."

She did howl.
And so did he.

They talked. They made love again, this time playing in the large glassed-in shower tucked opposite the tub.

They let Dancer out and let her in and finally got ready to eat lunch.

Rick stood in front of the refrigerator. He'd heard a lot of jokes about single women stocking only salads, diet pop and ice cream in their refrigerators, while single men had only beer and condiments. But the only time his refrigerator had ever been this bare was the hour between the delivery guys bringing it and him going to the grocery store. Nonfat yogurt, one-percent milk, egg substitute and fat-free salad dressing…what could you do with that?

"I can give you some of my candy bar treats."

He looked at her, looking entirely too innocent. "Those little one-bite wonders? No, thanks. Unless you want me to start stealing Dancer's food—" curled on the floor in the doorway, Dancer growled "—I need real food. Do you have a grill? Propane?"

She nodded.

"You actually eat something grilled?"

"Salmon. And zucchini and squash."

She could have salmon; he would eat steak. "Let's go to the store. Which one's closest?"

She told him as he trailed her out the door. She hadn't bothered putting on makeup yet—when had she had the time?—but it didn't seem to bother her going out without. And why would it? She was cover-model gorgeous with her naked skin.

The afternoon was sunny and warm with the humidity manageable. It would be a good time to spend three or four hours on the river back home. He couldn't catch any salmon for her, but he was sure he could land something she would eat.

But they didn't have time for a trip to Copper Lake and he hadn't yet convinced her that she might ever want to go. Maybe if he promised her Robbie's head on a platter.

It was a busy time at the shopping center. He found the closest parking space to the grocery store, only a half-mile hike away, grumbling about it as they walked.

"It's not even close to a half mile," Amanda admonished him. "Maybe tomorrow I'll make you jog to breakfast."

"Only if it's Waffle House and I get all-you-can-eat hash browns."

The interior of the store was cool, the aisles filled with shopping carts, adults and hyped-up kids.

She selected a few items for the cart—zucchini, yellow squash, carrots. He added onions and mushrooms and baking potatoes. She got bagged salad greens, three or four meals' worth, and he picked out tomatoes and cucumbers. He wasn't averse to eating salad; he just wanted something to make it good.

She bought wood chip cereal; he bought cheese danishes. She chose caffeine-free diet pop; he wanted the full-calorie high-octane stuff. She picked up vinegar for salad dressing; he got blue cheese with chunks the size of a golf ball.

"We are so incompatible," she said with a sigh as she steered the cart onto another, less crowded aisle.

"Nah. It's just that I see food as pleasure and nourishment and you see it as a test of willpower. But I don't like to drive the cart and you do, so there. Besides, have you forgotten what we did in the shower a while ago? You said it was physically impossible, but we managed, didn't we? Only two highly compatible people could have pulled that off."

Her cheeks turned the sweetest shade of crimson that extended down her throat and beneath the rounded neck of her T-shirt. And though the pattern of the shirt made it difficult to tell, he thought he saw the tiny point of an aroused nipple pressing against the cloth.

Laughing, he wrapped his arms around her, spun her around and gave her a smacking kiss on the mouth. "You're the best time of my life, Amanda. I'm going to be telling you that in grocery stores when I'm eighty-six and you're a sweet young eighty."

Another shopper passing by gave them an indulgent smile. So did the granny behind her. The third shopper didn't pass by. Didn't smile. Didn't do anything but stare at them, her mouth all pursed as if she'd sucked hard on a lemon.

Amanda stiffened and dropped her gaze to the basket of the shopping cart, fiddling with the keys hanging from a clip on her purse. Rick looked from her to the older woman and realized who it was. There was no family resemblance—Amanda looked more like her dad in the one picture he'd seen—but this store was less than a mile from Brenda Nelson's house and was the biggest and best-stocked grocery in the area. The surprise wasn't that they'd run into her, but that it hadn't happened before.

"Hey, Mom," Amanda said, her mouth barely moving.

"Amanda."

Rick frowned. He liked her name. It sounded sweet and funny and sexy and elegant and cool. But somehow Brenda turned it into three distinct, unforgiving syllables.

"How have you—"

"Are you still working at that place?"

"Yes, but—"

"Then you've got nothing to say that I want to hear." Brenda started to push her cart past, but Rick stepped in her way.

"Mrs. Nelson, I'm Rick Calloway, Amanda's—"

"I know who you are. You think I can forget one single high-and-mighty Calloway? You're Gerald's son. Sara's. Old man Jed's grandson. My husband, my daughter and I worked for you people, worked hard, and got paid a fraction of what we were worth. Your faulty equipment caused my husband's accident and when he was paralyzed, when he needed round-the-clock care, your grandfather said, 'Thanks for the twenty-one years of faithful service and get out of our house.'" She drew a deep, trembling breath. "Oh, I remember the Calloways. I pray every night for them all to rot in hell."

"Mom, Rick was a kid back then," Amanda protested. "He had nothing to do with the business."

Brenda treated him to a scornful examination. "He's no kid now. Bet he hasn't done a damn thing to change the way it's run."

"I don't work for the company, Mrs. Nelson."

"And where do you work?"

It would have been a better idea to let her pass when she tried. But Rick sucked it up and politely said, "Right now I'm tending bar at a club in the area, but I expect that to change before long."

Brenda laughed. "Tending bar? You're tending bar at the club where she dances naked? And your mother knows that? Oh, she must be so proud of you! Sara Calloway's oldest boy serving up drinks at a strip joint." The humor faded as quickly as it had come. "You two are a perfect fit. Trash and garbage."

She eased her cart forward and Rick moved to the side to let her pass. He watched until she was out of sight around the corner, then sighed. "Damn. That's one angry, bitter woman."

"You didn't pick up on that when I talked about her?" Amanda responded wryly. "I must have been too subtle."

She pushed the cart a few yards farther down the aisle, stopping in front of the condom display. As she studied the choices, he reached past her for a box of his favorite brand.

"Running into your mother in general counts as bad luck," he said, "but it could have been worse. She could have caught us here instead."

She picked a box of her favorite brand and tossed it in beside his. As she moved slowly toward the front of the store and the checkout, she casually asked, "What kind of job change are you thinking about?"

A case ended; another came along. But he couldn't tell her about that, so he shrugged. "My girl is starting a day job in January. Since her working all day and my working all night isn't conducive to great sex, I figured I'd change my hours, too."

He wasn't sure exactly what, but something about his words seemed to carry a pretty good emotional punch. She wrapped her fingers around his, pulled him closer and hugged him there in the checkout line.

If he could figure out what he'd said, he would say it again.

In private next time.

Chapter 9

When Amanda went to work that night, she took her own car. No need to advertise to everyone that she and Rick had spent the night together. If anyone saw them arriving with him only a few car lengths behind her, well, coincidences happen, right?

She was a little uncomfortable about walking into the dressing room for the first time—not because of Rick, but because of the scene Robbie had caused the night before. The noise coming from there indicated a full house tonight, filled both with regulars and girls who came by only now and then.

"How are you feeling, sweetie?" Eternity asked as soon as she set her duffel down.

"I'm fine."

"Let me see your arms."

Amanda dutifully held them out, and Eternity lightly touched the body makeup that made the bruises from Robbie's fingers virtually disappear. "Good job. Did you know that little putz was Rick's brother?"

"Yeah." Amanda grimaced. "Long story."

"You want to tell it sometime, Eternity will listen."

She'd already told it to the most important person last night. Amanda thought she might never need to tell it again. Before long, she might never even think of it again.

"Word is, after punching his brother in the jaw, Rick escorted him outside and little brother's face made contact with the hood of somebody's car nose-first. Boy's slow to learn when to keep his mouth shut."

After she turned six, there'd been no man to defend Amanda. Oh, the bouncers had occasionally pulled a guy away, but they were being paid to do it. And even though Rick had been getting paid, too, it had been personal with him. It had been about *her,* not the job.

And he'd called her *my girl.* She was surprised she hadn't swooned right there in the grocery store. The things he could do to her with nothing more than words...

"Where's Julia?" she asked after glancing around at both familiar and unfamiliar faces.

"She's already dressed. She went to get a bottle of water." Eternity leaned closer. "I tell you, I think this is all going to her head. She was asking me how to get invited to a special. There's one Friday night and she thinks she wants to go. I told her oh, no, she did not, but..." Eternity shrugged.

Amanda would tell her *oh, no, she did not,* and she'd bring Rick in for backup if she had to. Julia must be euphoric, reveling in her first real taste of feminine power. The trick was not letting it go to her head.

Amanda dressed in a thong, a flirty little side-split skirt, a bra and a sheer button-down blouse, all in black. Her shoes were black open-toe pumps with a wide rhinestone strap that circled each ankle. They were conservative enough for stripper shoes that, without the platforms, she would have been able to wear them to class in January. Oh, yeah, she thought with a smile as she admired them. Walking across campus and teaching class all day on seven-inch heels. Not only would it be hard on her feet and back, but it wasn't going to make it easy for the staff to forget her background.

There was no way to keep her background hidden from some people. If things got serious with Rick she would eventually have to meet his family and Robbie the moron couldn't be counted on keeping his mouth shut, no matter how many ways Rick told him to.

Well, she wasn't sleeping with Robbie, was she? Spending her time with him. Falling in love with him. Wanting a future with him.

Hearing the *L* word, even in her head, made her wince. She leaned close to the mirror to fix a smudge on her eyeliner and redo her lipstick, then straightened and pulled out the band that held her hair back. Curls tumbled around her shoulders, a wild coppery mass.

When she was a kid, her mother had found her hair too big a hassle, so she'd always kept it cut short. Rick liked it long. Liked running his fingers through it, watching the strands curl around. He liked stroking it when they lay quietly and he especially liked it when it tickled across his ribs and down his abdomen when she took him in her mouth. He tangled his hands in it then, arching, groaning harsh endearments.

Her face flushed so deeply that Eternity noticed. "You'd better get a cold drink before you go out on the floor. You look like you're going to burst into flames."

A cold drink. From the bar. "That's a good idea. You want anything?"

"No, thanks."

Amanda left the crowded dressing room behind and headed for the stage door. She'd been down this hall and halls just like it thousands of times. In the part of her that believed everything in her past combined to make her the woman she was today, she was going to miss them. Who knew where she'd be if she'd stuck to her original intention to make the dancing just a summer job? Would she have her degree and her upcoming job? Would she be living in the little house she adored? Would she be in love with someone totally different from Rick?

Probably not. She was beginning to think that Rick just might be her destiny. No matter what path she'd taken, it would have led her to him.

It was quiet in the bar, the only music coming from a small radio plugged in behind the bar. Chad was kicked back in a chair in the darkest corner, nursing a beer and waiting for seven o'clock to roll around. There was no sign of Vincent, who was tending bar with Rick tonight, and Rick and Julia were huddled close together at one end, their heads practically touching. If their expressions and hushed voices were anything to judge by, their conversation was intense.

Her and Rick's affair was so new that Amanda couldn't help but wonder if their discussion had anything to do with her. Had they decided they wanted to give each other another shot? Was Julia angry that he'd slept with someone else just days after they'd broken up? Were they discussing the best way for him to dump Amanda?

She would have given in to insecurity and backed through the door into the corridor again if Rick hadn't looked up and seen her. He didn't look as if he was planning to dump her. In her experience, that look was discomfort or guilt. He looked pissed.

Toothpick between his teeth, he jerked his head for her to join them. With a rush of relief, Amanda did so, stopping at the end of the bar where they leaned. He didn't kiss her, but his left hand slid from the bar and brushed her hip before settling at her waist. "Will you talk to her?"

Julia looked pissed, too. "I'm thirty-three years old. I don't need 'talking to.'"

"That's not what Eternity says," Amanda quietly disagreed.

"Eternity should keep her mouth shut. So should Rick. And so—" Julia bit off the insult before it finished. She started to run her fingers through her hair. "I'm an adult. I'm self-supporting. I don't need anyone's permission to volunteer for additional work."

"That additional work is prostitution, Julia," Amanda said flatly. "Having sex with men you've never seen before. And you don't even get to keep all the money. You want to do that? You want to let Harry sell your body to the highest bidder and pocket most of the cash?"

Julia stared mutinously at the bar, her mouth thinned.

"Have you ever even had sex with a stranger?"

"No. I missed out on a lot of experiences you had because I'm not as pretty or as popular as you. But I've had sex. I understand the mechanics. Whether for love or money, it's the same act."

"You're not doing it," Rick gritted out through clenched teeth.

Julia gave him a look only a few degrees kinder than a snarl. "You are not the boss of me. Not any longer. Not after the mistakes you've made."

Amanda looked from Rick to Julia. What mistakes? she wanted to ask. Had the breakup not been as mutual as Julia had said? But it must have been. She'd started trying to set up Amanda with Rick the same night.

"My mistakes are my own and I'll take responsibility for them," Rick said harshly. "But you are *not* doing any specials. Even if I have to handcuff you to that pole."

Julia looked at the pole on the main stage, then smiled sarcastically. "Ooh, Rick's gotten kinky since he started sleeping with strippers."

Amanda's entire body flushed. She couldn't decide whether to move closer to Rick or put distance between them, but he settled the question by drawing her to his side, moving his arm from her waist to around her shoulder. "Don't get bitchy, Julia, especially about Amanda. You wouldn't even be here if it wasn't for her."

"I know, I know. I'm sorry, Amanda. It's just…" Julia swiped at her eyes and her fingers came away damp. "Did you know there was a special last night?"

Amanda shook her head.

"I didn't, either. Apparently they filled it with girls from the other clubs except for one. Rica. She went and she's not coming back. Harry just told us she got a better offer."

Amanda's stomach clenched as Rick's arm tightened around her, then she swallowed hard. "She's just a kid. She's got a kid of her own. She's been saving money to move her daughter and her mother here from Augusta so they can live together as a family."

Across the room came a scrape of chair legs as Chad stood, stretched his arms high above his head, then started their way. Rick nudged Amanda and fixed his gaze on Julia. "Hey, I don't critique routines. Besides, when have you ever taken my advice about anything? I told you to buy a Mustang. You bought a Hyundai. I told you to give up cooking and you ruined every pan in my kitchen. You want advice from a man's point of view, honey, you're gonna have to find another man."

Chad set the empty bottle on the bar a few feet away, then leered at Julia from top to bottom. "Hey, sugar, I'd be glad to help you work on your routine. All you gotta do is ask."

Julia managed a more-than-believable smile. "I'll keep that in mind, sugar."

Chad sauntered down the hall that led to the bathrooms. A moment later came the brush of the men's room door swinging shut.

"We cannot just let Rica disappear," Julia said in a hushed, urgent voice.

"The next special's nearly a week away," Amanda pointed out. "If something's happened…it'll be too late.

Maybe—maybe she just decided to go home. Augusta's got strip clubs, too."

"I called her mother. She hasn't talked to her since Thursday and Rica hadn't mentioned any plans or changes to her."

Julia had called Rica's mother. Amanda had worked with the girl for two years and she didn't even know her real name. And yet Julia had known enough information to call Rica's mother. That was just…

"Rick, you have to do something. You have to call someone," Julia went on. "We can find out where the party was. Aren't they always held at one of a few places? We can send someone over there to look, to check it out, to talk to people in the area."

Rick looked at Amanda and swallowed a sigh. Julia was too emotional, talking too much, being too careless. In all the years they'd worked together, he'd never seen her as anything more than functional, competent, cool. She'd never been personally involved in a case, had never, ever talked in front of a civilian.

And she'd already said way too much to make Amanda suspicious.

"Julia." He snapped his fingers in front of her face. "I want to talk to you outside. Now. And—" he turned to Amanda and like that, his voice changed from stern to teasing "—since I'm guessing you didn't miss me that much in so short a time, I bet this is what you came up for." He produced a bottle of water from the bar refrigerator, twisted off the cap and handed it to Amanda. He circled the bar, took her arm in one hand, Julia's in the other, and guided them both to the back hallway.

Though she clearly would rather have gone with them, Amanda turned into the dressing room. Julia pulled her arm free and shoved the rear door open hard enough to make it bounce back. She stalked across the parking lot to her car, as competent in those ridiculous heels as the other dancers were, then spun around to face him. Before she could say anything, though, he did.

"Are you crazy, talking like that in front of someone else?"

"Are *you* crazy, sleeping with a woman that you don't trust to know who you are?" She thumped him on the chest, then threw both hands up with a growl.

"I trust Amanda."

"But you're not telling her the truth."

"Because I can't. You know that's not how these things work. You don't go around telling people that you're an undercover cop. It's a good way to get dead."

"You don't go around falling in love with people who are involved in your case, either, even on the periphery."

Rick couldn't argue with her, not about the impropriety of his actions or her assessment of his feelings. He *was* falling in love with Amanda. She was the best thing in his life.

But the timing sucked.

"Julia, I know you're worried about this kid. So am I. But we can't kick up a fuss right now. We've got nothing but suspicions and theories. If we do anything now, we'll blow this case."

"We've got four missing girls, and Angelita Moran is going to grow up wondering what happened to her mama if we don't do something."

Damn it, she was right. If Rica was still alive, wasn't keeping her that way worth blowing their investigation into the other girls' disappearances? "What do you want to do?"

"Amanda was right—the next party's too far off. Let me approach Harry. Tell him I need cash right away. I'm desperate. I'll do anything."

"And what if he asks you to prove it?"

She blanched, then stiffened her spine. "I'll deal with it."

"You can't *deal* with it, Julia. You can't do anything with these guys. You can't blow 'em, you can't have sex with 'em. Any case would be thrown out and you'd lose your job."

"That's okay. As long as we find Rica alive."

He stared at her. One time, after a particularly stressful day, she'd told him that her goal was management— the very top. And now she was talking about tossing away her career to save a stripper she'd known less than a week who *might* not even be in need of saving.

Before this case, apparently, she'd never known real stress.

She paced to the edge of the parking lot, then spun around, eyes alight. "How about this? I tell Harry that Rica told me she was working the special. She was a little worried because she'd heard rumors about girls disappearing after them. She told me if she didn't come to work tonight, I should call the police. I'm worried. If I could just talk to her and know she's all right…"

Rick was sure there were a dozen flaws with her plan, but it beat the hell out of her waltzing into Harry's office and offering to have sex with everyone who stood between her and Rica.

"What if he claims not to know anything?"

"He may claim ignorance, but he's not going to let me call the police. No strip-club manager wants the cops coming around, especially one who works for Rosey Hines."

"Instead of coming up with Rica, he could just make you disappear."

"Hard to do with this." Julia fingered a heart-shaped rhinestone clip in the center of her bra. "GPS. A gift from Carnie."

Rick had noticed the heart every time she'd performed, but hadn't thought anything of it. A lot of the girls added bits of glimmery jewelry to their outfits or chose a particular one for a statement. Eternity's was a quarter moon, and DinaBeth, the one who'd dotted her *i* with a star, had always worn shooting stars.

"The lab tech built a GPS unit into a pin for you?"

"Hello, we're working a case where strippers are disappearing. I'm a stripper. I'm a little more at risk here than you are." She shivered, more from the night chill, Rick suspected, than fear. After all, she wasn't exactly dressed for the weather.

Hell, she wasn't exactly dressed at all.

He unlocked his car door and grabbed a sweat jacket from the backseat. She put it on and gratefully tugged the edges together.

"Let's lay out what we know," she said. "Each of the girls apparently disappeared after doing a party for Harry. Tasha's and DinaBeth's cars turned up at one of

Rosey's chop shops. Lisa didn't have a car. Call in and have them put out a broadcast on Rica's car."

Pulling his cell from his pocket, Rick dialed their supervisory agent's number and did just that.

"There's no reason to believe the girls are dead," Julia said when she had his attention again.

"Beyond the fact that no one's seen or heard from them?"

"They were all reliable. Good moneymakers. Popular girls. Why would Harry or Rosey suddenly decide to kill them and lose that steady income?"

"Dancers are a dime a dozen," Rick pointed out.

"Good dancers? Who stick around, who show when they're supposed to, who love their job?" Julia shook her head. "You should hear the bitching in the dressing room. The missing girls were dream workers. Like Amanda and Eternity. They were happy here. There was no reason to kill them."

Killing your moneymakers was bad business, and if there was one thing Rosey wasn't, it was a bad businessman. "That rules out snuff films, too," Rick said. "You could grab a twenty-dollar prostitute off the street for that. And using them to pay off a debt. Again, you don't sacrifice your talent when a new girl would do just as well."

Julia scowled at him. "Hey, I made four hundred seventy-five bucks last night."

"And GBI thanks you." He leaned against the hood of his car. If he'd finished the paint job, he would smack anyone who did that, but there wasn't much he could do to mar primer. "Which means the likeliest theory is that Rosey's involved in some sort of sex ring. Either he's selling the women directly or he's providing them to a middleman."

"And that means they're probably going out of the country," Julia said. "To minimize the chances that they could escape or contact their families or get recognized by someone. And it would probably take a day or two to ship them out of the country." She paused, huddled inside the gray jacket. "Can I talk to Harry?"

The back door swung open with a thud and Vincent stepped onto the stoop. "Get your ass in here, Calloway. You're already freakin' late. I ain't working for both you and me."

"As if you could," Rick muttered, then called, "I'll be right there." To Julia, he said, "Call the SAC. Run it by him. If he says okay…"

He would. Rick knew it and Julia knew it. It was in the glimmer of excitement that shone in her eyes. She'd done a number of undercover cases, but none that put her in direct danger. She was getting off on the adrenaline rush.

It was giving Rick indigestion.

"Want my pistol?"

She scoffed. "Oh, yeah, where am I going to put it? But I'll take your cell phone."

He handed it over as Vincent bellowed again. "Be careful."

He crossed the parking lot with long strides, took the steps two at a time and smirked at Vincent as he pushed past. "What's the problem, buddy? Afraid you might actually have to work if I'm not there?"

"You know, I could get you fired."

"Maybe. How about if I hang out in the dressing

room while you try?" Upon a unanimous vote of the dancers, Vincent wasn't allowed in the dressing room. If he wasn't related to Rosey, he wouldn't even be allowed in the building.

"Get to the bar and start doing your freakin' job."

Rick stayed busy, though he managed to keep an eye on both doors that led to the rear and on Amanda when she came onstage. She was removing her see-through blouse, taking it one button at a time, when Julia finally came onto the floor. She smiled at a few patrons as she passed, but didn't slow to talk to any of them.

At the bar, she handed his cell to him. "He said to play it by ear."

"We got a receiver to track that thing?"

"Carnie's taking care of it. I'm going to see Harry now."

"Don't be accusing. You're worried, not suspicious."

She rolled her eyes and walked away from the bar.

Rick didn't like this. He was used to being the one in danger. He could handle it. Julia was smart, but without a weapon, she was pound for pound weaker than any of Harry's goons. Maybe, if she got into trouble, she'd remember Amanda's example of kicking Vincent in the balls.

Maybe, if God smiled on them, she wouldn't get into trouble.

Rick rubbed his left foot against the pistol strapped to his right ankle. He trusted in God. He also trusted in being prepared in case God was otherwise occupied.

Amanda's flirty little skirt came off in the next number, and she was doing amazing things with the stripper pole, but he was too distracted to feel more than a twitch of lust. *Do you think Amanda's in danger?* Julia had asked last week.

Would her friendship with Rosey keep her safe? It damn well better or there would be hell to pay.

What if another girl disappears before we find out what's going on? Julia had asked in the same conversation, and she'd answered for both of them. *We live with it.*

Funny how things could change in so short a time. Julia's involvement in the case. Rick's involvement with Amanda. One thing he knew for certain: the three of them—they *would* live.

He couldn't say the same about anyone else involved.

Amanda was due for a break and she wanted nothing more than a little time with Rick. Since he'd taken his break a few minutes earlier—with Julia—she settled for time alone, where she could puzzle out the confusion in her mind.

Why had Rick started asking questions about Tasha and the other girls? Why had he been convinced that something had happened to them one moment, then the next repeated back her own explanations to her? Why did he really carry a gun? How had Julia really come across that photograph of the girls? Why was she so upset about Rica supposedly taking another job? How had she known Rica's mother's phone number? Why had she asked Rick to send someone over to the party location, to check it out and talk to people in the area?

That sounded like something cops did.

Being curious about girls who might have disappeared. Carrying a gun when it could not only cost you your job but land you in jail. Knowing a lot of information and even having photographs of people who interest you. Being so upset when your kid brother comes around when you mentioned the club name only one lousy time. Knowing how to find someone's real name and her mother's name and phone number. Being able to call that mother out of the blue and get information from her.

Cops.

Rick and Julia.

Amanda reached her private closet, swung the door in, and it stopped halfway. It was Rick's shoulder that blocked it. He glanced at her, then moved aside, leaving enough room for her to step in.

Barely enough, because Julia was already in there. Though Rick smiled, it didn't reach his eyes, and Julia didn't even make the effort.

"Am I interrupting something?"

Mouth set in a tight smile, Julia shook her head.

"We were just talking," Rick said. "Old stuff."

A few minutes ago, Amanda might have been jealous. A few minutes ago, she'd have believed that "old stuff" was the affair they'd shared. Now she doubted that they'd ever seen more of each other than they did here at the club.

Now she believed they were working together, insinuating themselves into the club, making friends with the dancers, gathering information. Willing to do anything to get it. Perform at one of Rosey's special parties. Sleep with the dancer who'd been around longest, who'd known all of the girls. Use. Deceive. Pretend.

Rick slid his arm around her, then nudged the door shut. "Are you on break?"

"Yeah."

His mouth brushed her forehead and she realized that she didn't care. Didn't care that he'd used her. Didn't care that the past few weeks had been a pretense for him. Didn't care that he and Julia had lied to her and everyone else.

Well, of course she *cared.* At some point in the future, she was probably going to care a whole lot. Her heart was probably going to break.

But she'd gotten something, too. Fabulous sex and, more importantly, companionship. He'd spent time with her, talked to her, listened to her, and he hadn't paid to do it. He might have done it as part of his job. And she'd *liked* spending time with him, talking and listening. It was the closest to a normal relationship she'd had in twelve years, and if she could manage it with him, she could manage it with someone else.

Once her heart was finished breaking.

"Well…" Julia moved, shifting around to the side. "Aren't we a bundle of fun? It's almost time for my set, so I'd better go…" She maneuvered her way to the door, then looked back at Amanda. "I'm sorry I got bitchy earlier. You're a good friend, Amanda."

After the door closed behind her, Amanda leaned against the wall where Julia had stood. "That sounded almost like goodbye."

"Nah. Julia's not going anywhere."

"But Rica did."

"Julia asked Harry about her. He said he's got a new number for her but doesn't remember where he put it. He'll have to find it."

Amanda nodded. She wished she had put her shirt and skirt back on or, better yet, stopped in the dressing room to borrow Eternity's red satin robe. She would rather not feel quite so naked…though there might not be enough clothing in the world to make her feel secure at this moment.

The urge to nibble on her fingernails, a nervous habit she hadn't done since high school, was so overwhelming that she folded her arms across her middle, then tucked her hands behind each elbow for good measure. "Rick…you're not really… Tending bar isn't…" Grimacing, she took a breath and blurted out, "You and Julia aren't really—"

He cut off the rest of her words with a kiss, quick and hard. When he lifted his head, he stared down at her, his eyes dark with intensity. "Please don't ask that. Not yet."

He held her gaze until she slowly nodded, then he glanced at his watch. "I've got to get back to work. If Vincent has to come looking for me again, he's gonna be pissed."

She smiled weakly. "Vincent's always pissed."

"I'll give you a ride home tonight."

"But my car—" She broke off and nodded. If he gave her a ride tonight, then he'd be around tomorrow to bring her back to her car. It was pathetic, but it was something.

She sat out the rest of her break in the small room, zoned out, unable to think or even rouse herself until she heard Eternity's voice down the hall.

"Amanda? You back here? There's a customer out front asking for you."

With a little shake to pull herself together, she left the

closet and returned to the floor. She caught a glimpse of Julia, onstage, and another of Rick behind the bar, but she kept her focus on the customer Eternity pointed out.

Focus—that was how she got through the rest of the night. Three o'clock seemed way later than usual. She was weary to her bones, in a way that the job never affected her. It was a good thing she was getting out in four weeks. She felt whipped.

The dressing room was a crowd of women, some discussing their plans to go out and party, others looking as if they'd been out past their bedtimes. She changed into jeans, a sweatshirt and her beloved Crocs, then went looking for Rick. She didn't have far to go. He leaned against the wall at the end of the hall.

"Has Julia already left?" he asked, holding his hand out to her as she approached.

"I don't remember. I'll go back and look."

He opened the door, then shook his head. "Nah, her car's gone. She said she was going to try to get out early."

The chill made Amanda shiver and he wrapped his arm around her shoulders, snuggling her close against him for the short walk to his car. He opened the door for her, waited for her to settle in the seat, then closed it again. Things, she thought, that he'd never done with Julia; things that had made their affair less than convincing.

Things that made his affair with Amanda very convincing, when it wasn't real, either. She was the *mistake* Julia had ridden him about earlier that evening. Had his goal been to befriend her, romance her, seduce her, but stop before actual sex?

The car smelled of him. His scent was in the jackets

in the backseat and permeated the old leather of the seats. It was in the very air and she closed her eyes, breathing it in deeply.

The smell intensified when he climbed in beside her. She followed his actions by sound—the buckling of his seat belt, the turning of his key in the ignition, his boot leather creaking on the clutch, the shifting into Reverse.

They'd driven a couple of blocks in silence before she felt his glance. "Am I still welcome at your house?"

She smiled. "Anytime."

"Do you mind if I stop by the apartment and pick up some clean clothes?"

"And make sure Julia got home safely?"

She sensed his shrug. "Of course not," she said.

A very large speed bump marked the entrance to the apartment complex. She opened her eyes then and saw that more of the streetlamps were out than on. Music thumped from a car in a side lot, its headlights off, and the small gang of men gathered around it turned to watch them pass.

"I used to live in places like this," she murmured.

"Here? Or in Copper Lake?"

"Both—though minus the thugs in Copper Lake. The biggest threat there were the Holigan brothers."

"My granddad called them the Hooligans. I was buddies with a couple of the older ones for a while."

"Really? I didn't know Calloways were allowed to be friends with anyone from the north side of town."

His mouth tightened. "Amanda—"

"I'm sorry. You didn't deserve that." Robbie may have been an arrogant snob. Granddad and the uncles were definitely haughtier-than-thou, and the women were exactly as her mother had described them that morning—high and mighty. Except for Sara. And Rick. He wasn't like his family.

He turned the corner into the back parking lot and swore. "Julia's car isn't here."

Amanda glanced at the second-floor apartment. Only one dim light burned in the living room. "Would she have gone anywhere after work?"

"Not without telling me."

Amanda quietly pointed out, "She left work without telling you." He may have known that Julia wanted off early, but she hadn't stopped by the bar or called his cell and said, *I'm leaving now.*

He parked and took the stairs in leaps. By the time Amanda stepped onto the bottom one, he was wiggling the key in the lock, then shoving the door open. He dropped his keys, where a table used to be, she assumed as she picked them up, and he charged down the hall. She remained inside the doorway, keys wrapped tightly in her palm, until she heard the creak of shoe leather behind her, along with the shuffle of fabric. She started to spin around, but a hand grasped her shoulder and something hard and dangerous-feeling poked against her back.

The man holding her nudged her forward and she took a few stuttering steps. "Rick?" she said, trying to keep her voice steady.

The only response was upheaval in Julia's room. Had another man been waiting for him there? Should she be looking for a weapon, thinking about escape instead of being too frightened to think straight?

"Rick! You have company out there."

Running thuds in the hall, then he skidded to a stop at the corner. "Get your hands off her, Tyrone, you moron."

"Hey, we weren't sure she was with you."

"If you didn't see her get out of my damn car, you should have."

Amanda moved to the safety of the dining table to study the three men. Tyrone wore jeans and a Falcons shirt. The older man was in a suit, complete with tie, at three-freakin'-thirty in the morning, and the third guy— ratty jeans and T-shirt, unshaven, habitual scowl, eyes murky dark—looked like *he* should have been the one working undercover with Vincent, not Rick.

Rick disappeared a moment, then came back in, a gun holstered on his belt. It was much bigger and deadlier-looking than the one on his ankle. As he slid a black case into his hip pocket, he gestured toward the small group. "Where's Carnie? She was supposed to be handling the GPS tracker."

The older guy lifted one hand in Amanda's direction. "I'm sorry, Miss Nelson, but would you wait in one of the bedrooms?"

She looked around. Tyrone was gazing at the ceiling, Mr. Tall, Dark and Sleazy didn't care either way and neither did Rick. Because he would tell her everything he could when they were gone?

Politely she nodded and passed Rick into the hallway. It had sounded as if a battle had gone on in Julia's room, but it had merely been Rick tearing through things looking for information. Clothes were scattered everywhere, from thongs, breakaway skirts and bras to staid, boring business suits and everything in between.

Instead Amanda turned into Rick's room across the hall. The furnishings were Spartan, no books, no custom-rod magazines, no pictures. Of course, this wasn't his home. He'd been slumming on the wrong side of town. He probably had a great condo, or maybe his brother had built him a house, complete with garage for working on the car. That was the place he would take women who were *really* a part of his life.

While she was part of his lie.

The apartment walls were thin, allowing her to hear a rumble of voices from the dining room, but she couldn't distinguish any words. She peeked out the door and saw that Rick had moved, joining the other men at the table. She eased down the hall, past the other bedroom door, hesitating at the darkened kitchen before turning in. There was a small pantry between the wall and the refrigerator, and she pressed herself hard against the pantry door to listen.

"—when Dautrieve didn't show up, we called Carnie." That was the suit talking. "Carnie located her car in a parking lot a mile and a half from the club off Calhoun. Her clothes, her, uh, outfit for the night, was on the backseat and her purse was on the floorboard. Her cell was inside."

"We know she wouldn't leave the GPS transmitter behind on purpose." Deep, sexy rumble, had to be the sleaze with the scowl. He probably cleaned up really well, but he was dressed just fine for the scum he was dealing with now.

"So someone made her undress and they took her from there." The suit sounded very pragmatic, given that it was one of his employees who'd been taken somewhere naked. "We're in the process of getting warrants for the club, the chop shop, Harry's and Rosey's houses, plus a short list of the others."

"That'll take too much time," Rick said. "We're pretty much agreed that Rosey's shipping the girls out of the country, right?"

"Well, his cousin did buy a container shipping company out of Savannah a month before the first girl disappeared and he's had movements two days after each girl disappeared."

Amanda could see the scowl in Rick's voice when he said, "Yeah, Tyrone, thanks for sharing that with us *yesterday* when it could have been really useful. And it's not just our girls who have disappeared?"

"Three dancers from Savannah, four from Macon, four from Charleston, six from Jacksonville," said Mr. Dark and Sleazy. "There are probably more."

"All young girls who meet certain specifications. That's probably the reason for the special parties, so the buyers can select the girls they want. The oldest one so far is—"

"Twenty-three," Dark and Sleazy said in his deep, sexy rumble.

"Julia is thirty-three. And she didn't get grabbed from a party. She went to the boss obsessing about a missing girl and talking about calling the police. They didn't grab her to add to their shipment—"

"Though that's always a possibility," Suit said.

"They grabbed her to keep her quiet. To keep the cops away."

To kill her. Amanda's knees went weak.

"What's your point, Calloway?" Suit asked.

"By the time you get warrants and we round these people up and persuade someone to talk…"

"She's gonna be dead," the dark guy said flatly.

"What do you suggest I do? Let you go in there and kick Harry's ass?"

"No," Amanda said, startled for an instant that she'd spoken aloud. But since she had, she moved out of the corner and walked into the dining room, stopping next to Rick's chair. "I'd suggest that you let someone Harry knows really well make a trade for Julia and Rica."

The suit folded his arms over his chest. "And what is it you think Harry would want that badly? You?" he asked skeptically.

"No." She dipped her knees in a bend familiar from the stage as well as the floor and straightened with Rick's wallet in her hand. She flipped it open and held it out so everyone could see. "A cop. On his payroll. Harry would want that really bad. Trust me."

She was absolutely right. There wasn't much that would please Rosey, and therefore Harry, more than to have a traitor handed over on a silver platter. And there wasn't anyone at Almost Heaven, Rick thought, who could make Rosey happier for doing the handing. He liked Amanda. He actually considered her a friend. It wouldn't occur to him that she could be more dangerous to him than his worst enemy.

Supervisory Agent Baker fiddled with his tie, Tyrone and Evan discussed the details of backup, more GPS devices, multiple surveillance vehicles, ready to head to any part of Atlanta on short notice. Amanda was wired— Rick had done it himself with equipment brought up from Baker's car—and now they were just waiting.

Rick stood at the living room window, his shoulder bumping Amanda's, gazing out as she was. It had started to rain a few minutes earlier, the steady kind of fall that was more nuisance than anything. It washed dirt off the cars in the parking lot below and made the blacktop gleam.

"Everything looks better through rain," she commented.

"Are you sure you want to do this? It's dangerous."

"Lucky for me, I know a couple of GBI agents."

"When did you figure it out?"

"This evening."

"You'll have to tell us later where we screwed up. Julia and I have never worked undercover together like that."

Amanda's glance flickered his way. "She could already be dead."

"No. Intellectually I know that's possible, but in my gut— No." The only people who got killed on his cases were the bad guys, and even that was rare. When it came right down to it, most people wanted to live, even if it was in prison.

"You ready to go?" Evan asked, talking to Amanda. He was going to follow her back to Almost Heaven, to listen to her conversation and get her the hell out of there if something went wrong.

"Yeah." Her smile was wobbly and her fingers when

she squeezed Rick's hand were icy. "Can I borrow a jacket from Julia so I don't get soaked?"

"Sure."

She went to the coat closet and sorted through them before settling on a trench coat that was so not her style. It covered her practically to her ankles and belted around her waist, and it had a hood that swallowed her and a fake cape sort of thing across the back. She pulled the hood forward until her face was nothing but shadow, then started toward the door.

Rick grabbed his own slicker. "I'm going, too."

Baker started to protest, but Evan nodded. As long as Evan wasn't seen—and he was the best at not being seen—then Rick wouldn't be.

Amanda climbed into the Camaro, started the engine and slowly backed out. He was surprised she could drive a stick shift, but why not? She did a lot of things her peers couldn't do.

Hell, she didn't even have any peers.

Evan was driving a beat-up van, with enough dents to make a body man rich, a broken antenna, taillights missing their covers and taped over with red plastic and a cracked windshield. He followed her at a distance, turning into the business just before Almost Heaven and circling to the rear where a row of scraggly bushes between parking lots gave some cover.

Amanda parked near the back door of the club. Harry's Cadillac was in its usual space. It was habit for him to stay after closing on Saturday nights and do the books and the liquor inventory, according to Amanda. He usually finished about the time the Sunday-morning cleaning crew arrived, and he let them in before leaving.

It wasn't routine for Rosey to be there, as well, but his stretch limo was parked nearby. It appeared empty.

Looking small and insubstantial in the too-big coat, Amanda climbed the steps and opened the rear door with her own key. The instant it closed behind her, Rick's stomach knotted. He hadn't apologized to her yet, hadn't told her he loved her, hadn't tried to talk her out of this. He was letting her walk into danger. No matter that she'd volunteered, he should have stopped her. But for Julia's sake…

He was just like his brother, using Amanda for his own purposes. But all Robbie had hurt was her pride. Rick could cost her her life.

The receiver picked up footsteps, doors opening, then Amanda's voice. "Hello? Harry? Rosey, are you here?"

"Amanda, is that you? Come on in here. Take off that wet coat and have a seat." Rosey sounded genuinely happy to see her, though he must be wondering what had brought her out at four-thirty in the morning.

"I'll keep the coat, but I'll take the seat. Harry keeps this place frigid."

"Gotta cool off the customers."

"How's your mother?"

"She's in Tahiti and loving it. She's staying in a little cabin on stilts above the bay and says it's wonderful. Huh. When we visited my uncle Ernest years ago and stayed in his fishing cabin on stilts above the bayou, that wasn't so wonderful. But pay a thousand dollars a night for it, and it sure looks a lot better."

Amanda laughed, sounding as natural as ever. "I bet Tahiti doesn't have the mosquitoes Uncle Ernest had."

"And Uncle Ernest didn't have the Jacuzzi tub, the satellite TV and the air-conditioning."

There was a pause, then Harry spoke for the first time. "If the chitchat's done, what brings you out so late, Amanda?"

"I heard about Rica."

"Yeah, well, you've been in the business long enough to know that girls move on. Hell, you've moved on like that a few times yourself."

"I also heard about Julia. That she was threatening to go to the police about Rica and now she's just gone, too."

Neither Rosey nor Harry spoke.

Wishing for video to go with the audio, Rick stared at the building. It was pretty much deserted, with only Harry and Rosey inside and Rosey's driver outside. Maybe Baker had had a good idea when he'd popped off about Rick kicking Harry's ass. The man was past sixty; Rick could take him. As for fat Rosey, he'd just shoot his ass, grab Amanda and get the hell out.

And in a few days, maybe a few weeks, they would find Julia's body dumped somewhere.

"Listen, you guys know I'm quitting in four weeks," Amanda said.

"Yeah, to take a job at that fancy college. One of our own hittin' the big-time." Rosey sounded like he was smiling. "I'm proud of you, Amanda."

"I'm proud of myself...as far as that goes. Not so much about other stuff. I know what's been happening with the girls. Rica, Tasha, DinaBeth, Lisa. I know it's happening to other clubs, too, in Charleston and Macon and Savannah. I know these parties are kind of a sales party. You provide the girls, the buyers look them over, even try them out, and choose the ones they want. And then they're moved, probably out of the country."

Neither man made a sound.

"I've known for a while, and truth is, I really didn't care. Until you took Julia. I want her back. And because Rica is important to her, I want her back, too."

There was a long silence, two, maybe three minutes. Rick admired Amanda's courage in waiting it out instead of getting shaken and starting to ramble.

"What is Julia to you?" Rosey asked at last.

"She's my protégée. I taught her everything she knows. I brought her here to dance. I told her this was a good place with good bosses. And she's my friend."

That was a nice touch, Rick thought, especially when she must be wondering if anything about Julia had been based in truth. He and Julia had both misrepresented themselves to her and she must have a few doubts.

"You've been here a long time, Amanda. You've made a lot of money for us. But why would you think we would just turn over two girls to you—if we even have them?"

"Because I have something that's worth so much more."

"And what would that be?" Harry's voice was gravelly, as if he'd talked too much recently. Having one of his girls threaten to bring the police down on his establishment could certainly necessitate a lot of conversation.

"I don't know if you're aware that Rick Calloway and I have been…involved."

"I don't care what you do with the help as long as it's not on my time."

"Yeah, you should talk to Chad and Dawn about that. There's a reason we knock on doors around here."

Rick grimaced. "I thought I was the only one unlucky enough to have walked in on that."

"So what about you and Calloway?"

"He's a heavy sleeper, and when he sleeps, I like to look around. And look what I found."

There was a rustle of movement, then the thud of Rick's credentials case hitting the desk. A chair creaked and Harry swore.

After a time, Rosey spoke, his voice soft. "Georgia Bureau of Investigation. Didn't we have a little trouble with them before?"

"Yeah, at the chop shop. They raided the place in Covington."

"So, Amanda, where is Calloway right now?"

"I'm not telling. But I'll bring him to you. You have Julia and Rica there waiting. We'll make the trade."

Another silence, broken by the sound of ink on paper. "Okay. You bring him to that address in two hours. We'll make the trade."

"Rosey, we've got a deal with—"

Rosey's voice thundered. "He's a damn GBI agent! In my club! I don't give a damn about the deal you made for some little whore. Find another girl to fill the order and turn these two over to Amanda."

Rick continued staring hard at the club, hardly

noticing the rain. Each second lasted minutes, punctuated by goodbyes, then footsteps. Down the hall. Around the bar. Along the back corridor. Out the door.

Relief made him weak as Amanda got into his car and, a moment later, drove away. She turned onto the street and drove past them without looking, but murmured, "The meeting is at a salvage yard north of here. It's going to take thirty minutes to get there."

That gave them ninety minutes to plan.

Good thing he worked well under pressure.

Amanda slowed well ahead of the turnoff and switched the windshield wipers to a lower setting. "How long does it take to put a plan like this together?" she asked,

Slumped in the seat beside her, Rick grinned. "As long as you've got, darlin'. They give you an hour, you damn well better have something worked out in an hour." Then he turned serious. "You don't have to do this. It's not too late. Just pull over, get out and walk away. I'll turn myself in to them."

"Of your own free will? They'll know something's up. They'll—" She paled, and a little gasp escaped her as the car bumped from the highway onto the well-worn dirt drive of the salvage yard.

They would kill him, unless he did some damn fast talking. He thought he might succeed—he'd talked himself out of tighter places—but it wasn't just his life at stake here. There was Julia's and Rica's...and Amanda's.

A hundred feet into the yard, a vehicle parked in the middle of the road began slowly moving forward. "I guess I follow him." She sounded hollow. "Where are all your fellow cops?"

"They're as close as they can be." They had some of the best snipers around out there, including Evan. *Close enough* could be a mile away on a good day, less in the rain.

"Gee, that makes me feel safe."

"I'll be right there beside you, darlin'. And if you manage to keep that weapon hidden from them…" It wasn't a great chance, but he'd learned that any chance was a good one. "Amanda."

Gripping the steering wheel with both hands though she was driving no more than fifteen miles an hour, she looked his way. They were both wired for sound; God knew who was listening, but he didn't care. "My old man never had anything to do with why I never got married. I was just waiting for you."

Her eyes widened, the fear chased away for an instant. She opened her mouth, closed it again…and the road suddenly turned, opening into a clearing. Headlights lit the early morning gloom, turning the rain silver. The lead car stopped and so did she, keeping her death grip on the steering wheel.

"Shift into neutral, shut off the wipers and the headlights and turn off the key," Rick said quietly.

Like an automaton, she obeyed.

Rosey's Mercedes was parked on one side of the clearing, and he stood beside it, wearing a trench coat that could have sheltered a small family with his weaselly driver holding a huge umbrella over him. Behind them was a small metal building, an office or storage of some sort. Rick counted eight men, including Rosey, Harry, Chad and Vincent. All but Harry were armed.

"I'm betting Julia and Rica are in the building," he murmured. "I'm only seeing eight, including Fat Boy and his driver, but there are probably more."

Usually *I-talk-you-listen* was Rick's favorite method of communication with these guys, but he would have liked a little feedback this morning. After all, he *was* getting ready to face a bunch of people who wanted to kill him with no armor, no pistol, not even a damn rock he could throw.

"You ready?"

Amanda, still pale, nodded and opened the door, stepping out into the rain, sweeping the hood up over her head. Rick climbed out, too, but left his slicker hood hanging. "Mr. Hines," he greeted cheerfully. "Amanda tells me you have a proposition for me."

"Mr. Calloway. I apologize for these conditions."

"A little rain never hurt anyone."

"So I've heard." Rosey gestured and several of the men holstered their weapons and came forward. "You won't mind if my men search you and then we'll get inside out of this mess and talk business."

Two of the men searched Rick, turning him so he leaned on the hood of the Camaro, and did a piss-poor job of it. Tough guys like these never liked to thoroughly search another tough guy's crotch. When they finished with him, they stepped back a dozen feet, and the third man, Vincent, moved closer with his oily grin.

"Gotta search you, too, Amanda," he said, practically

salivating over the opportunity. He reached out, and she took a step back, one arm outstretched to stop him.

"You touch me, Vincent, and I'll kick your balls out through your nose this time." Slowly, ever the performer, she pushed the hood off her head and lifted her hair free of the coat, exposing it to the rain. Even more slowly, she pushed the sleeve off her left arm, raised that hand to the opposite shoulder and worked that sleeve off, too. Gripping the coat by the collar, she walked forward a few feet as if on a catwalk, turned slowly, arms out from her side, then strolled back to the Camaro.

Every man was stricken into silence. She'd insisted on stopping at home to change clothes before coming here. The white pants she'd put on gave new meaning to the words *low rise*. Rick couldn't imagine the pair of panties that could hide within the scant inch or two of fabric that made up the front and seat of the pants. Her top was white, too, a simple T-shirt that ended some-where north of her belly button and clung to her very nice, very bare breasts. The chilly rain made her nipples pucker and the thin material clearly showed the rosy brown shadows that circled them.

Rick's tongue was too thick for his mouth. Aw, man, he'd never, ever gotten turned on in a life-or-death situation, but he was throbbing in places where he shouldn't be.

"Good enough, Rosey?" she asked, striking a pose, her voice throaty and promising all kinds of fantasies.

"Good enough, Amanda. You see why she's my number one dancer. Shall we get down to business?"

With a smile and a wink, she shrugged into the coat

again, pulling the front edges together and tying the belt tightly. "We shall. I've lived up to my part of the bargain. Now it's your turn."

"Wait a minute," Rick said. "What bargain? You said he was interested—" He turned to Rosey. "I thought you wanted to make a deal with me."

"Not with you. For you." Rosey gestured, and the two men who'd searched Rick raised their weapons, pointing them center mass at him.

"But—hey, come on—I make the club run easier for you. That idiot—" he pointed at Vincent "—is almost as lazy as he is stupid and the girls hate him. They like me. And I can do more. I can help with your other interests. I've just been waiting for a chance."

Rosey reached inside his pocket, then flicked his wrist. Rick's credentials landed open in a mud puddle about six feet in front of him. "I bet you're interested in *all* my interests, aren't you? The clubs, the girls, the auto parts, the shipping. Even just my shipping enterprise could keep the Georgia Bureau of Investigations busy for a long time. But *your* interests aren't in *my* best interests. So…" He shrugged.

The two men started moving, but Amanda stepped in front of Rick. Her heart was racing, her stomach was heaving and she was so cold that she couldn't feel her toes. But she stood her ground, hoping she looked half as cool as she was trying to. "The trade, Rosey."

Again he gestured, and the door to the metal building creaked open. Julia stumbled out first, barefooted, wearing a man's shirt that hung to her knees. She was dazed and there was a smudge on her cheek that was probably a bruise. She looked around numbly, until she recognized Rick, then reached behind her and pulled out Rica. She still wore her stripper clothes from Friday night, with only another man's shirt to provide protection against the fall chill.

Amanda hoped Julia was dazed enough to not realize what was going on. If she understood her life was being traded for Rick's, she would refuse and might take some action that would get them all killed.

"Julia," Amanda called. "Rica. Come over here."

Rica took a few wobbly steps. "Amanda? Is that you? Oh my God!"

"It's me, guys. Come on over here behind me. It's okay."

The two women had practically reached them when Julia saw the badge case lying in the mud. Her steps faltered and she looked from Rick to Amanda. Whether it was the look he gave her or Amanda's silent prayers, though, she kept moving, kept Rica moving.

"All right, Amanda," Rosey said. "You've got your girls. Give us our cop."

Behind her Rica gasped and Julia whispered, "You can't—you can't—what the hell are you doing?"

"Do you mind if I say goodbye?" Amanda asked. When Rosey shrugged, she took the few steps necessary to reach Rick. He turned his head so her first kiss brushed his jaw and whispered in her ear, "Evan's about ten feet to my right. Get them behind the car."

Smiling, she slid her hands into his hair, gripping his head, holding him for a desperate, hungry kiss. After an instant, his arms slid around her, fumbling for the holster secured under the capelet across the back of the coat. He pulled the weapon free with his left hand, shoved her away and shot the nearest of the two men who had intended to kill him.

Rica screamed as gunfire erupted around them. Amanda darted around the car and helped Julia drag the girl to the rear of the vehicle, shoving them both to the ground. She yanked the coat off and spread it over the three of them as if it would somehow protect them and she prayed.

"Oh, God, oh, God, they're gonna kill Rick," Julia repeated over and over.

Amanda slapped her hand. "Dear God, they're *not* gonna kill him." She hadn't told him yet that she loved him, hadn't said that if those words in the car—*I was just waiting for you*—were a proposal, the answer was absolutely yes, because she'd just been waiting for him, too.

Glass shattered nearby—the rear window of the Camaro, Amanda thought as pieces rained down on the trench coat. There were shouts, curses, shots so loud that they made her ears ring.

Then everything was quiet. Rain fell, splashing in puddles. Rica whimpered. Amanda's harsh breathing mixed with Julia's.

Either Rick and Evan and their backup, wherever they were, were down, or Rosey and his guys were. And since her heart was still beating, her world hadn't just suddenly ended, Amanda knew which it was. She eased the coat from her head and flexed tight muscles to rise from her place in the mud. Before she'd done more than clear the trunk of the Camaro, Rick grabbed her, pulling her into his arms, trying to wrap her inside his coat with him.

"You're all right, you're all right," he whispered. "Oh my God." Brushing wet curls from her face, he kissed her forehead, her nose, her cheek, before thrusting his tongue into her mouth. That quickly, the chill was gone, heat bubbling through her veins with arousal and pleasure and love. *Love...*

She freed her mouth from his and cupped her hands to his face so she could stare intently into his eyes. "I love you."

"I know."

"And I'm going to marry you."

He grinned. "I know that, too. And we'll have beautiful daughters who will kick the asses of Satan's other grandspawn."

People were arriving, sirens sounding, voices approaching, but Amanda's focus was entirely on Rick. "I never thought I'd say this, but I can't wait to go back to Copper Lake and meet the rest of your family."

"Really? You'd do that for me?"

Her brows arched. "I just came out half-naked in the cold rain, put on a show and pretended to turn you over to a man who wanted you dead. Yeah, I think I can stand a few days in Copper Lake. As long as you don't mind if I kick Robbie's balls out through his nose."

Rick laughed and pressed his face into her wet curls. "Aw, darlin', you are definitely the girl for me."

Epilogue

Copper Lake didn't look anything like Amanda remembered. Granted, it had been fifteen years since she'd left, mourning her father and heartbroken over Robbie, and towns changed. But even the places that remained the same—the square, the river that meandered through the middle of town, the schools, a few stores—all seemed brighter. Less depressing. Less threatening.

She sat quietly in the passenger seat of the Camaro, gleaming in the November sun with its new cherry-red paint job. The damage done in the shoot-out had been mostly cosmetic and Rick had patched it up on the days he'd taken off that following week.

Patched it, patched her. They'd made love, talked, planned and just been together. Doing yoga before breakfast while he watched, handing him tools when he worked on the car, sharing his couch—deeming hers too uncomfortable for snuggling, he'd moved his in along with the rest of his stuff—and watching TV... God, it sounded so schmaltzy, but the old saying was true. Life's simple pleasures were the best.

He reached for her hand, twining his fingers through hers, making the diamond in her engagement ring send sparkles dancing around the car. "You okay?"

"Yeah." There was nothing in Copper Lake that could hurt her. Sure, there were Calloways who weren't thrilled to have a girl from the north side of town joining their family, and then there was Robbie, but they weren't important. Rick loved her. That was all that mattered.

"Anyplace you'd like to see?"

She glanced at the clock. They'd left Atlanta around seven-thirty that morning to beat the Thanksgiving traffic. With Almost Heaven and the rest of Rosey's clubs shut down, and him and half his family in jail awaiting trial, she'd taken advantage of her joblessness to get accustomed to the hours a respectable college instructor would keep. It hadn't been as easy as she'd expected, but Rick helped, waking her every morning before he left for work so he could say a very sweet goodbye.

"Just the places where you grew up."

"What about the places where you grew up?"

She thought about them—the shabby houses and apartments, the logging company where her dad had worked, the succession of diners and low-rent stores where her mother had worked. The schools where she'd been a nobody until Robbie had brought her to everyone's attention. The lumberyard where her summer job had brought her to *his* attention. The hospital, the doctors' offices, the church she had attended on occasion…they weren't important, either. She would never forget the people, places and events, but she would never regret them, either.

"I know my history," she said. Life might not have been easy, but it had made her who she was today and she was very proud of that woman.

"Okay. One quick tour of the life and times of Rick Calloway in the grand old town of Copper Lake," he said with that easy grin she loved, and made a U-turn on River Road, the main drag.

She knew some of the places, of course—the schools. The elegant-columned church his family had founded, then attended for two hundred years. The football field, named for his uncle Jeb, where he'd been a star. The baseball diamond next door to the high school, where he'd played out a lackluster career. The SnoCap Drive-In, where kids with time and money to spare had hung out, and Charlie's Custom Rods, where he and his brothers had honed their appreciation for old engines.

A few were new to her—his favorite fishing hole on the river north of town. The back section of his grandfather's land where they'd hunted for sport. The country club where he'd attended the prom his junior and senior years. She could imagine what he must have looked like, charming and handsome in his tux, enjoying high school and anticipating college, carrying an absolute conviction that life would turn out well for him. He was a Calloway; it couldn't possibly be anything else.

Finally he followed River Road north out of town, past the turn to his mother's home, another half mile past the main entrance to Calloway Plantation. He turned onto a narrow dirt lane and followed it to its end, a clearing on the banks of a creek.

Amanda climbed out of the car and met him at the front. He reached automatically for her hand; she gave a little squeeze as his fingers closed around hers. "Another fishing hole?"

He shook his head.

"A place where you brought your girlfriends to make out?"

"Nope. You're the first girl I've ever brought here. This is my land. Granddad gave each of us kids five acres. Robbie's is a couple miles that way—" he nodded to the east "—and Russ's is a mile north. Russ lives on his." Chuckling, he wrapped his arms around her and snuggled her close. "Don't worry. I've never wanted to live in Copper Lake. But this would be a nice place to visit, don't you think? To bring our kids for weekends away from the city?"

She nodded. "Teach them to fish."

"Tell them stories about their mama."

"Who will retaliate with stories about their dad."

"You can grade papers while I fish. I'll clean 'em and you can cook."

She smiled at him, warm and happy and, for the first time ever, absolutely certain that life would turn out well. She was in love with and loved back by the best man she'd ever known. "Ha. You can teach me to fish, and whoever catches the fewest does the cleaning *and* the cooking. Sharpen up your kitchen skills, darlin'."

He snorted. "I'm a damn good fisherman."

"So was my dad. It's in my blood."

Laughing, he lifted her off the ground and turned until the rough bark of a tree was at her back and his body, warm and hard, was against her front. "You're in my blood," he murmured, brushing kisses across her face before reaching her mouth. "God, I love you."

God, I love you, too. She didn't know if she said the words out loud and didn't care. He knew, because *he* was in *her* blood, too. They connected to each other. Completed each other.

"Russ will build us a house if you're interested." A pause. "Are you?"

Amanda looked around. Tall, slender pines stretched endlessly into the sky; their needles and cones carpeted the ground. The creek bubbled from small falls into a pool, clear and deep, and the only sounds that disturbed the quiet were the birds. The breeze. Their breathing.

Amanda Nelson, from the wrong side of town, living in a house on Calloway land, married to the handsomest, sexiest and best Calloway of all. What would her father think of that?

She knew the answer to that in her heart: as long as she was happy, he would be happy. That was all he'd ever wanted for her.

"Oh, yeah," she said, smiling up at Rick. "I'm interested."

* * * * *

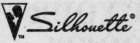

Silhouette®

Romantic
SUSPENSE

**Sparked by Danger,
Fueled by Passion.**

When Tech Sergeant Jacob "Mako" Stone opens
his door to a mysterious woman without a past,
he knows his time off is over. As threats to Dee's
life bring her and Jacob together, she must set
aside her pride and accept the help of the military
hero with too many secrets of his own.

Out of Uniform
by Catherine Mann

Available February wherever you buy books.

SRS27571

REQUEST YOUR FREE BOOKS!

2 FREE NOVELS PLUS 2 FREE GIFTS!

Silhouette® Romantic

SUSPENSE

Sparked by Danger, Fueled by Passion!

SRS07

Texas Hold 'Em

When it comes to love, the stakes are high

Sixteen years ago, Luke Chisum dated
Becky Parker on a dare…before going
on to break her heart. Now the former
River Bluff daredevil is back, rekindling
desire and tempting Becky to pick up
where they left off. But this time she has
to resist or Luke could discover the secret
she's kept locked away all these years….

Look for

TEXAS BLUFF

by Linda Warren

#1470

*Available February 2008
wherever you buy books.*

HSR71470

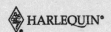

Romantic
SUSPENSE

COMING NEXT MONTH

#1499 CAVANAUGH HEAT—Marie Ferrarella
Cavanaugh Justice
It's been years since Chief of Detectives Brian Cavanaugh has seen his former partner Lila McIntyre, and he's surprised to discover their chemistry is as hot as ever. But he banks down his emotions in order to help Lila catch the stalker who has been harassing her...and discovers a secret that threatens their lives.

#1500 MATCH PLAY—Merline Lovelace
Code Name: Danger
OMEGA undercover agent Dayna Duncan jumps at an undercover assignment overseas. What she doesn't expect is to find former lover USAF pilot Luke Harper awaiting her arrival. A forced reunion may be the only way Dayna and Luke can keep up their aliases, but can they withstand their attraction long enough to complete their mission?

#1501 OUT OF UNIFORM—Catherine Mann
Wingmen Warriors
When Tech Sergeant Jacob "Mako" Stone opens his door to a mysterious woman without a past, he knows his time off is over. As threats to Dee's life bring her and Jacob together, she must set aside her pride and accept the help of the military hero with too many secrets of his own.

#1502 THE PASSION OF SAM BROUSSARD—Maggie Price
Dates with Destiny
A hot lead on a cold case homicide teams up Officer Sam Broussard and OCPD sergeant Liz Scott. Although Sam has never met Liz, there's something very familiar about her. While they uncover the mysteries surrounding the murder, Liz and Sam discover a past neither one remembers sharing...and a killer bent on separating them for eternity.